GOING OFF SCRIPT

GOING OFF SCRIPT

JEN WILDE

Swoon READS

New York

A Swoon Reads Book

An imprint of Feiwel and Friends and Macmillan Publishing Group LLC
175 Fifth Avenue, New York, NY 10010

Our books may be purchased in bulk for promotional, educational, or business use.
Please contact your local bookseller or the Macmillan Corporate and Premium Sales
Department at (800) 221-7945 ext. 5442 or by email at
MacmillanSpecialMarkets@macmillan.com.

Library of Congress Control Number: 2018955585
ISBN 978-1-250-31127-6 (hardcover) / ISBN 978-1-250-31128-3 (ebook)

Book design by Aimee Fleck

First Edition, 2019

10 9 8 7 6 5 4 3 2 1

swoonreads.com

To all the queer folks who won't
be buried, hidden, or erased.

Thank you for being exactly
who you are.

CHAPTER ONE

The door of the bus hisses as it folds open, and a burst of warm air swirls around me. I heave my suitcase down the steps and squint through the glare bouncing off the sidewalk.

I'm here. I'm actually in Los Angeles. After spending years daydreaming about this moment, it's happening. And it's even better than I imagined, because this is real. The sun is burning my pale skin, the smell of freshly brewed coffee and exhaust fumes fills the air, and I'm kicking myself for thinking my fave plaid shirt was a smart outfit choice in this weather. But it's all okay, because I made it.

I open Google Maps on my phone and check the street signs. I've stared at the map of West Hollywood so many times in the last few months that I could probably find Parker's street in my sleep, but the part of me that likes to be in control needs to have the map ready, just in case.

"Okay," I say quietly to myself. "I'm on Santa Monica Boulevard. Good."

I start walking, dragging my suitcase with its one busted wheel behind me. It's Sunday afternoon, and there's a chill vibe in the air. Tattooed people in printed shirts and oversize sunglasses sip cocktails at trendy outdoor cafés. Locals stroll along the sidewalk, and I smile at their dogs. Bars are painted turquoise and lemon yellow, and there's so much stunning street art that I don't know which one to Instagram first.

I can see why Parker, my cousin, loves this neighborhood. Its Old Hollywood vintage-style neon signs and proud queer culture are a perfect fit for him. Compared to our gray hometown of Westmill, Washington, it's like being on another planet.

Just as I'm thinking of home, I get a text from my mom.

Mom: are you there yet? Let me know you're safe xo

I'll reply later. There's too much going on here that I don't want to miss, and if I'm honest, the last thing I want to do right now is think about home.

That town was suffocating me. Closing in on me like the walls of the trash compactor on the Death Star. I made it out just in time to avoid being crushed by the weight of utter normalcy and conformity. Being here feels like breathing after holding my breath my whole life. I'm free. Free to be exactly who I've always wanted to be.

While waiting at the famous rainbow crosswalk, I arch my back to stretch out muscles that are still stiff from being stuck on a bus for eighteen hours. If I were anywhere else, I'd want to find a place to shower and nap and recover from my journey, but not here. All I want to do is dump my suitcase and start exploring this town. The air is filled with limitless possibility that gives me a buzz when I breathe it in.

This is where people who love creating fictional worlds as much as I do all gather to make magic. The world's most iconic stars have been born here. My heroes have walked these streets.

Emotion swells in my chest, and I squeeze my eyes shut. I can't believe I actually made it.

Finally, I can stop dreaming and start doing. No more long, rainy nights standing behind a deep fryer, feeling a thousand miles away from where I wanted to be. No more hiding in the back of classrooms, counting down the days on the calendar until I could be free.

I'm here for an internship on my favorite TV show: *Silver Falls*—about werewolves and the people who love them. This time tomorrow, I'll be sitting in the writers' room, taking notes and listening to ideas and trying not to fangirl all over everyone. I'm about to take my first big leap toward my goal of creating my own TV show. I'll intern this summer, hopefully find a job as a personal assistant to a showrunner, then work hard and pay my dues for a while. After a few years, I'll be promoted to writer. My days will be spent crafting story lines and creating characters I've always wanted to see on my television. Then, maybe by the time I'm in my thirties, I'll have proven myself worthy of getting my own hour of airtime. I'll be Bex Phillips: showrunner.

That's my plan, anyway. Mom always says, "Every house needs a blueprint and every dream needs a plan."

I check the map on my phone again. One more block. I look up just as two pretty people with long legs and colorful hair walk by. One wears a T-shirt with HELLA BI printed on it, and the other has a denim jacket covered in buttons that proudly support trans pride. They don't notice me staring at them— they're much too infatuated with each other. They hold hands and giggle as they walk by, and I'm filled with such hope and joy that all I can do is swoon.

I'm home.

When I turn down Parker's street, I still can't wipe the smile from my face. It's lined with palm trees. The sky is a perfect blue. I feel like I've stepped into a postcard. But the closer I get to his building, the higher my nerves rise.

I made it to LA, which means there are no excuses now. Is it possible that some part of me believed I'd never actually make it this far? Did I feel safer holding on to a dream that was so huge, I never thought it would ever come true? What do I do now that it has?

I mean, it's not like I'm the first eighteen-year-old stepping off a bus in LA, carrying a suitcase full of dreams. Everyone has heard those stories of young hopefuls flocking to Hollywood, chasing fame and fortune. But this town is notoriously tough on new arrivals. I could get eaten alive. I could end up back in Westmill with my tail between my legs and my dream crushed to smithereens. God, the jerks from school would love that.

My heart starts racing. Sweat drips down my back, and I'm not sure if it's from the California heat or my sudden burst of anxiety.

Limitless possibility . . . that's a lot of pressure.

Walking the streets of my heroes . . . that's a lot to live up to.

Stop dreaming and start doing . . . that's a lot of responsibility.

Jesus. This is actually happening. I'm here. It's all on me now.

I cannot fuck this up.

CHAPTER TWO

"Come on, dude, be nice," I mutter under my breath. "Please."

I'm talking to a door. An orange door with a faded green *16* nailed onto it, just above the peephole. And I'm talking to it because no matter how hard I try, it. Won't. Open. I slide the key in for the fifth time, jiggle it, twist it, but it doesn't budge. My fingers sting from trying to turn it.

"You mother . . . ," I grunt, then stop myself and take a deep breath. It's too damn hot for this. I drop my backpack on the welcome mat and sit on my suitcase.

I pull my phone out and text Parker.

Bex: Cuz. I think you left the wrong key under the mat.

Parker: what?

Bex: Your door won't open.

Parker: one sec

I hear footsteps coming up the steps, and a moment later, Parker appears. "Hey!"

No.

No, he's not supposed to be home yet.

I was supposed to shower and unpack first.

He was supposed to come home and I'd be there, clean and fresh and awake and with the words "I'm gay" on my lips.

"I thought you had clients all day?" I ask.

He pulls his makeup case behind him, the wheels rolling loudly across the concrete. "I fudged a little. I wanted to surprise you!"

"Oh," I say. "Yay!" I push my disappointment aside so I can just enjoy seeing him after so long.

Last time I saw him in person, he was boarding a plane from Seattle to LA, his forehead glistening from nervous sweat. That was three years ago. He'd just graduated high school and was moving to Hollywood to train as a makeup artist. Now he's glowing. And somehow, he still looks eighteen even though he's almost twenty-two. His skin is bronzed from the California sun, and his teeth are whiter, but he's still my dorky cousin. I can see that from the tears in his eyes.

"I told you," he says as he pulls me in for a bear hug. "I said you'd make it here one day, and here you are!"

"Here I am," I say with an excited smile. He holds me at arm's length, taking in the sight of me.

"I'm so glad you stopped straightening your curls," he says as he tugs on the ends of my shoulder-length hair. It's red, like his used to be before he bleached it white.

"Don't get too close to me," I say, shaking my hair loose from his fingers. "My stench might attach itself to you." Spending all night on a bus with busted air-conditioning never smells good.

He cringes and pulls his keys from his pocket. "I wasn't going to say anything, but yeah." He slides his key into the door. "There's a trick to this bitch. Watch and learn."

I take note as he pulls the handle toward him, jiggles the key, and kicks the bottom corner of the door. It opens with a thud and a creak.

"That seems overly complicated," I say as I swing my back-pack over my shoulder.

Parker shrugs. "Welcome to LA."

I follow him inside, dumping my bags onto the cushion-covered futon that will be my bed for the next month, at least.

Parker twirls in the middle of his living room. "So what do you think of my bachelor pad?"

The outside of the building is old, faded pink and stuck in the seventies, but the inside is modern, sleek, and very Parker.

Framed black-and-white photos of Old Hollywood adorn the cool gray walls: Marlon Brando, James Dean, Sidney Poitier. A metal bookshelf holds framed Polaroids of Parker and his friends in between stacks of books by makeup artists like Kevyn Aucoin and Bobbi Brown. He works freelance as a makeup and hair stylist, mostly on the Glamsquad app, but recently he's been getting jobs prepping celebs for award shows and photo shoots.

"I've never slept on the futon myself," he says. "But Ma slept fine on it when she came down to visit, and you know how fussy she is."

I chuckle. "She wanted me to give you this, by the way." I pull him in for another hug, squeezing him tight around the ribs. My aunt Laura is a big woman and super strong, and her hugs damn near break you, but in the best possible way.

"Aww," Parker says as he squeezes me back. "I miss that old girl."

Should I just tell him now? Is this the moment? *Just say it, Bex*, I tell myself for the thousandth time. *I'm gay. I'm gay. I'm gay.* I open my mouth and wait for the words to come out, but my voice seems to be hiding. Just like me.

Logically, I know I shouldn't be so nervous to come out to him. It's not that I'm afraid he won't accept me—he will. But I've spent my whole life doing whatever Parker did. I looked up to him. When he started school, I threw a tantrum because I wanted to go to school, too. When he got the training wheels off his bike, I made my mom take mine off, too—which ended with me upside down in a bush, but I didn't care. I wanted to be like Parker so much that it became a running joke in our family and earned me the nickname Lil P. I think the rock in my stomach that's weighing me down and stopping me from biting the bullet is the fear that they'll laugh at me. That Parker will give me a sympathetic smile and brush it off as another way I'm trying to be like him. Or Mom will laugh her loud, throaty laugh, shake her head softly, and say, "Aww, Lil P. That's cute." Or the kids from school will think I'm coming out to be relevant and gain attention.

I just don't want to be laughed at.

Maybe I could just add it nonchalantly to the end of any sentence, like it's no big deal. I could say something like, "I'm tired and I'm gay." Or . . . "I've missed you and I'm gay."

"Oh! Wait," he says, and takes his phone out of his jeans pocket. "I promised your ma that I'd let her know when you arrived."

He opens the camera on his phone and holds it up to take a video of us.

"She's here, Auntie Jack!" he says.

I wave to the camera and smile. "Hey, Ma! I'm alive! You can stop worrying now!"

Parker stops recording and texts the video to my mama. It's Sunday afternoon, so she's at work with my old crew at the

Westmill Sonic Drive-In. Right now, she's probably stuffing burgers into bags and wrangling staff together for the lunch rush. It's wild to think that I was right there with her a week ago, rushing orders out to cars and getting soaked in the Seattle rain. And now I'm here, sunburned and sleep-deprived in Los Angeles.

Parker points behind me to the kitchenette. "The kitchen is too tiny for any kind of mess, so eat whatever you want, just clean up your shit." It's super small, but super neat and organized. He walks over to a closed door and pushes it open. "My room. You have to walk through here to get to the bathroom."

Some people might think this is too small a space for two people, but Parker and I have shared a room our whole lives. I'm actually kind of excited to be living with him again. It'll be just like when we were kids, only now we won't have to whisper the day's gossip to each other so our moms don't hear.

"I cleared space behind the mirror for your meds," he says. "You're still on Ritalin, yeah?"

I nod. "And Lexapro now, too."

He raises his hands to the air. "Same, girl, same."

I could say it now. Just spit it out. He's queer as hell. He'll understand. Shit, he'd throw me a party.

I feel it coming. The two most important words of my life are rising up inside me like an air bubble rising from the bottom of the ocean.

"Parker," I say. My heart feels like it's stopped, like it's listening, waiting for me to introduce it to him from behind an invisible curtain.

"Mhmm?" he says as he clicks open his cosmetics case.

I can't do it. I'm chickening out. I don't know how to say the words. I just keep picturing him laughing in my face the moment I do. The air bubble pops before it reaches the surface, and I slouch onto the futon. My eyes feel heavy, and suddenly all I want to do is sleep. But I can't stand the smell of myself, so I dig my bathroom bag out of my backpack.

"I'm gonna have a shower," I say.

"Sure thing, honey," he says with a smile.

I start walking to the bathroom when he calls my name. When I turn around, he's got tears in his eyes again.

"I'm so glad you're finally here."

I give him a tired smile. "Me too."

And I'm gay.

CHAPTER THREE

"We need to leave Silver Falls," Jonah says as he wraps Tom's arm in gauze.

Parker and I are watching the new episode of *Silver Falls*. At the end of last season, a family of werewolf hunters came into town and have been causing havoc ever since, so tonight Jonah and Tom are hiding out in an old barn just outside of town. The buzz online is that the queer YouTuber and actress Alyssa Huntington is joining the cast as a special guest tonight, but the episode is almost over and she hasn't made an appearance yet.

"No," Tom growls, still struggling to keep his werewolf side under control. "I won't be chased from my home. I'd rather die."

"Then you will die," a new voice says from offscreen.

I grab Parker's hand and we both squeal in anticipation as Alyssa emerges from the shadows.

Onscreen, Jonah jumps to his feet, standing between Alyssa and Tom, his teeth bared. "Who are you?"

The camera zooms in on Alyssa just as she says, "I'm one of you."

The credits roll, and Parker and I bounce excitedly on the futon.

"You have to introduce me to Will Horowitz," Parker says as he squeezes my hands in his. Will Horowitz is the actor who plays Jonah, and Parker has had a crush on him since season one. "I promise I'll thank you at our wedding."

I laugh. "He's got a boyfriend. Ryan from that band the Brightsiders."

Parker groans. "Fiiiiine. I'll take Archer, then."

"He's straight, I think."

"Oh," he says with a pout. "Well, you should date him, then. It's about time you got yourself a cutie like him."

My cheeks burn. "Ha. Yeah. I don't think fraternizing with the talent is on my list of intern duties."

Also, I'm gay.

Parker takes our plates of half-eaten macaroni and cheese into the kitchen. "You gotta tell me if Alyssa Huntington is staying for the whole season. It's about time they added another queer kid to that show. Six seasons and only one gay is not enough."

I nod. "I hope the character she's playing is queer, too."

Parker puts the plates in the sink and claps his hands

together. "Let us pray," he says with a sigh, like he's asking the Gods of Gay to make it so.

. . .

The next morning, I'm in the passenger seat of Parker's old Buick LeSabre. Its blue paint is faded and the interior is torn and stained from all his morning coffees, but it works, so that's all that matters to me. There was a time when neither of our moms could afford a car, so being able to drive anywhere we want still feels like a luxury to us. Even in LA.

The radio plays the latest Bleachers hit, and the sun is already turning up the heat even though it's not even 8:00 A.M. yet. I feel like a bowl of Jell-O, jiggling and shaking as the car rumbles through the traffic. I'm so nervous for my first day that I couldn't eat breakfast, and now I'm sweating through the navy button-up shirt that I so carefully picked out just for today.

Parker catches me sniffing myself and pops open his glove box. "I got you." He pulls out a spray-on deodorant and I quickly stuff it under my shirt and apply it.

"Thanks, man," I say.

Soon, we're pulling up at the entrance to the studio lot, and my heart is pounding out of my chest. A tall bronzed arch towers over the entry, with *Rosemount Studios* engraved into it. To think that some of the most legendary performers, writers, and directors have passed through these gates over the decades, and I get to follow in their footsteps. I snap a photo and send it to my mom and my best friend, Gabby, while Parker pulls into the line of cars waiting to pass security at the gate.

My phone buzzes with a text from Gabby.

Gabby: GOOD LUCK TODAY BABE

Gabby: send me tons of pics! xo

Gabby is pretty much my only IRL friend. We went to high school together and basically started hanging out because we were the kids the bullies picked on most. We bonded over fanfic and music and spent most of our time reposting each other's Tumblrs. We're like sisters, but even she doesn't know I'm gay.

Bex: so nervous. Gonna die.

Gabby: lol wanna trade? Summer just started and I'm already bored out of my mind.

Bex: I'll take it

Gabby: stfu! This is everything for you.

I feel like a traitor to my own dreams for this, but I honestly would trade with Gabby right now. She's got the summer off before college. Days of sleeping in, sitting in front of the television, and doing nothing sounds pretty damn appealing as I sit here in a hot car, so anxious it feels like my heart is about to explode. I squeeze my eyes shut and imagine I'm home, in my bed, safe under my covers. No responsibilities, no pressure, no way to fail. But when I open my eyes again, I'm still here. And I'm terrified.

"I can't do this," I say.

Parker smirks like he was waiting for me to say that. "Yeah. You can."

I shake my head. "Nope. This was a bad idea. I'm not ready for this. I'm just a child!"

He bursts into laughter. "Bex, you're eighteen. You're grown. You can do this."

"Nope," I say again. "Nuh-uh. Turn around. I wanna go back to Westmill. I'm not ready to be grown."

He stops laughing and turns to look at me. "Honey, this is all you've been dreaming of since you were seven and I took you to see *Twilight*. I'm not letting you leave."

I fold my arms over my chest. "Okay, firstly, bringing up my *Twilight* phase is a low move. Secondly, maybe I'm not ready to achieve my dream just yet. I'll try again next year."

The guard lets one of the cars ahead of us in and we move forward in the line.

"What are you gonna do in Westmill for a year?" Parker asks. "Work at Sonic with your ma every day and go home and write *Silver Falls* fanfic all night?"

"What's wrong with that?" I ask, offended.

"Nothing!" he says, his voice a couple of octaves higher. "If that's what you really want. But that's not what you want. You want to go into that studio and be the best fucking intern in the history of interns. You want to schmooze the higher-ups and hustle your way into a job writing about hunky werewolves."

My stomach does flips and I wrap my arms tighter around myself. "I'm gonna barf."

He shrugs. "So barf. You wouldn't be the first one to puke in this car. But then you're still going to march into that writers' room and do the job you fought so hard for."

He's right. I did fight hard for this opportunity. I worked almost every day after school and on weekends for nearly two years to save up enough money to come to LA. I stalked all the social media of television studios and signed up for every newsletter and joined every Facebook group to find writing internships. I filled out dozens of applications. All while trying to pass my classes and graduate high school. I promised myself that it would all be worth it once I made it through these gates.

Another car is let through. There's only one car ahead of us now.

I let out a sigh. "I hate you."

"Awww," Parker says teasingly. "I hate you, too, sweetie."

When it's our turn, I introduce myself to the guard, an older gentleman with glasses and thinning white hair, and tell him I'm here for my internship and show him all my IDs and paperwork. The pages tremble in my hands, and the guard gives me a warm smile. His name badge says PETER, but he tells me I can call him Pete as he welcomes me to the studio. I like him already.

The gates slide open, and we drive into the lot. I feel like I'm entering a lost city of magic and wonder, like when Thor took Jane to Asgard for the first time in *The Dark World*.

Parker pulls into the visitors' parking lot and gives me a hug. "Now, get out and have a blast."

"Thanks, P," I say.

My fingers shake as I open the car door and step out. The phrase "fake it till you make it" repeats in my head, and I try my best to play it cool. I hold my head high as I enter the building, but the door makes an awful creaking noise that makes everyone in the reception area stare at me. Totally thrown off my game, I bypass the front desk, hurry as casually as I can into the gender-neutral bathroom, and lock myself in a stall. I'm sweating again, so I tear some toilet paper off and wipe my armpits with it. Stains are already forming on my shirt. Note to self: Do not lift arms at all today.

After a minute or two of deep breathing and fanning my sweaty spots with my hands, I swing the door open and step back out, taking what Parker said to heart: If I need to barf, I'll barf, but then I'm going to get back up and keep going.

I've got a dream to chase.

CHAPTER FOUR

"Room 121. Room 121. Room...," I mutter to myself as I walk down the hallway, checking the numbers on all the doors. My new official lanyard hangs around my neck, swinging slightly with each step I take. I reach the corner boardroom, with a sign on the door that says ROOM 121: SILVER FALLS WRITERS' ROOM. Just like Angela, the cute girl at reception, described.

I take a moment to compose myself. Deep breath in, slow breath out.

Time to go for what you want, Bex.

I knock on the door, but all I get in response is silence. Someone walks out of the office behind me and down the hallway. I try to smile at them, but they don't even notice me. I knock again. Still no answer.

Do I knock for a third time? Maybe they're saying come in but I'm just not hearing it. Should I just go in? Ugh, I feel like such a loser. I touch my fingers to the door handle, turn it an inch, and wait, listening. Still nothing.

"Um, hello?" I open the door, hoping I'm not interrupting anything.

I'm greeted by an empty room.

"Hello?" I say again for good measure.

Weird. Angela said they would all be here. I take one last look down the empty hallway and step inside the room. A long table sits in the middle of the room with eight office chairs around it and a tin of whiteboard markers in the middle of it. A couch sits along the far wall, under a window that overlooks the staff parking lot. But the thing I can't take my eyes off is the whiteboard on the wall behind the table. It's covered in Post-it notes and paragraphs of dialogue and ideas for the latest episode. I step farther into the room and see the wall to the right of that plastered with headshots of the cast, along with their character names and more Post-it notes. A long timeline is pinned above them, listing all the pivotal moments from season one to season six—the current season. There's the episode when Jonah's girlfriend, Katie, died. Ugh, I cried so hard that night. And the episode when Tom led the other werewolves into war with the vamps. That was one of the best episodes to date, in my opinion.

"Can I help you?" a voice asks from the doorway. I jump out of my skin like I've been caught doing something I shouldn't be.

The guy stares at me, waiting for my answer.

"Hi," I say with a smile. "I'm Bex, the new intern."

He cocks his head to the side. "I wasn't aware we were getting a new intern this season."

I hold up my lanyard. "Oh, well. I'm supposed to be working in the writers' room with Malcolm Butler."

He makes a face, like he just got a whiff of something bad. "I'm Malcolm Butler."

I narrow my eyes at him. He doesn't look like Malcolm Butler, at least not like the photo on his Twitter profile. But the longer I search his face for the resemblance, the more I see him. He looks older, with more lines around his eyes and gray in his hair, and a scruffy beard.

Shit. I can't believe I didn't recognize *the* Malcolm Butler. He's been the showrunner since season four and a leader in the industry since before I was born. My cheeks warm in embarrassment.

For some reason, I wave. "Hi! It's so nice to meet you! I'm a huge fan!"

He does a cool kind of chin nod and drops his satchel on the table. "We're about to have a meeting to go over the next script."

Oh my god. I'm about to listen to the writers of *Silver Falls* talk about the latest script.

OhmygodOhmygodOhmyfreakinggod.

"Cool," I say, trying to seem as casual as possible. But I can't stop grinning. I sit on one of the chairs at the table but instantly realize I've fucked up when he looks at me like I've offended him.

"No," he says. "The writers sit at the table."

I stand up so fast I push the chair into the wall, and one of the cast photos falls off.

"Oh my god, I'm so sorry!" I gasp. I scramble to pick up the headshot and pin it back where it was, all while he watches and sighs and very definitely starts to loathe me already. Then I walk to the other side of the room and stand there sheepishly.

We wait in unbearable silence for a little while. I look everywhere but at him. Nervous sweat runs down my back.

"You look young for an intern," he says, narrowing his eyes.

It's not a question, but the suspicion in his voice pushes me to give an answer. "I'm getting college credit."

He nods. "UCLA?"

I rub the back of my neck. "Community college."

"Look," he finally says. "I don't normally allow interns in the room. But Ruby—the new network head—wants us to . . ." He pauses and does air quotes with his fingers. "'Lift as we climb,' like this is some diversity outreach program instead of a business. Anyway, she's the boss, and lucky for you that means you can stay."

"Thanks," I say, even though I'm a little offended.

"Before everyone else gets here," he continues, "tell me, do you have any relatives in the business?"

"No," I say. "My family is small. Just me, my mom, aunt, and cousin. Oh, wait, actually, my cousin is a makeup artist."

"Oh," he says, like he's finally interested. "Which studio does she work for?"

"He," I say. "And he's freelance. Mostly makeup and hair for photo shoots."

He lowers an eyebrow. "So no one in the film or television business, then."

I shake my head. "I guess not."

He opens his laptop but keeps asking questions.

"Do you have any interest in writing?" he asks.

My eyes light up. "Oh, yes."

"Do you intend to have a career in television writing?"

"Yes," I say. "That's always been my dream."

He chuckles. "*Dream*. You're one of those. Well, I hope you're serious about this. I don't want to waste anyone's time here," he says. "If I'm going to let my writers take time out of their own jobs for you, I need to know that you're going to work hard. I'm not interested in giving you an 'epic fangirl experience.'" He uses air quotes again. "You have to take initiative and prove that you're in this for the long haul."

I stop smiling and put on my serious face. "I'm very serious. I want this more than anything."

He taps his pen on the table a few times. "Well, good. Do you have any writing experience?"

I tug on the sleeves of my shirt. "I've been writing on

FanFic.com for years. My most popular story there has over two million reads."

"FanFic.com." He says it with a judgmental tone, then turns his attention back to his laptop.

I feel myself getting defensive but rein it back in. "I've also written scripts, and obviously I had to write scenes and episodes for my internship applications."

"Obviously." There's a pause as he starts typing on his laptop. "You didn't submit to any scriptwriting contests or fellowships?"

I deflate a little. "No." I don't want to tell him that I couldn't afford any of the entry fees, so I leave it at that.

"Hmm," he says. "Well, I expect you to be here five days a week. Lunch breaks are thirty minutes."

"Yes, sir," I say quietly. My stomach turns uneasily. The application said this was supposed to be a Monday-to-Wednesday gig. I was planning to get a part-time job, so I'd be earning some money, seeing as this is an unpaid internship. But he's my boss, and if he says I need to be here Monday to Friday, that's what I have to do. I'll just have to stretch my savings and go over my budget again. Ugh. My chest tightens with panic just thinking about it.

Just then, a short guy with spiked-up hair and a laptop walks in. He walks by me and takes a seat on the couch.

"Dirk," Malcolm says. "You're late."

"I know, I know," he says. "I've been searching everywhere

for the fountain pen you wanted, but it's sold out everywhere. Even online."

"Don't whine to me," Malcolm says, rolling his eyes. "Just do your job. And fix that attitude. You're dropping the ball lately."

Dirk just nods, and then they sit in awkward silence, with me standing near the door and wondering if I should leave the room.

Finally, other people arrive. Some make eye contact with me and nod; others don't seem to even notice I'm there. I'm disappointed, but not surprised, to see that there's only one woman at the table, and everyone is white. I hope I'm not the only queer person, but I'm not going to hold my breath. I wait for Malcolm to introduce me, but he just starts the meeting.

"Happy Monday, folks," he says. "Let's get straight to it. Andy, what have you got for us?"

A guy wearing a gray hoodie and black-rimmed glasses hands copies of his script around the table. He glances at me, then at the last script in his hands, then looks at Malcolm like he's unsure of whether to give me one.

"Oh, right," Malcolm says. "This is our new intern."

Everyone in the room turns to look at me, and I rub the tips of my sneakers together nervously. I wonder how I must look to them. Broad-shouldered girl with orange curls, thick glasses on the edge of her nose, sweat-stained shirt, and black jeans. I try to muster a few ounces of confidence, but it's not enough to even make eye contact with anyone.

"Hi," I say to my shoes. "I'm Bex."

Everyone smiles and says hi, and Andy hands me a copy of the script. "Just FYI," he says. "That's top secret, so don't, like, take any selfies with it or anything."

I nod. "I won't. It's safe with me."

My fingers trace over the paper. I want to cry. This must be how Gollum felt when he held the ring.

"Oh, Becky," Malcom says. I consider correcting him about my name, but I'm so intimidated that my words get stuck.

I guess my name is Becky now.

"I'd love a coffee," he says. "Run over to the café, would you? Anyone else want one?"

Others in the room start listing their orders, and I frantically type them out on my phone.

"Got it," I say. "Be right back."

"Thanks, doll," Malcolm says as I walk out the door.

Doll? Ugh. I'd prefer Becky.

CHAPTER FIVE

By the time I return with their orders, the meeting is wrapping up.

"Oh," Malcolm says when he sees me. "I was wondering where you'd gone."

"Sorry," I say as he takes his cup off the tray in my hands. "The line was out the door." And also I got seriously lost. This studio is bigger than all of Westmill.

The other writers take their cups off the tray as they walk out the door. They all thank me, which is nice. My phone vibrates in my back pocket, and I strategically fish it out while still holding the drink tray. It's my mom. Ugh. She knows how important this day is for me; why is she calling now? Doesn't she know how embarrassed I'd feel, taking a call from my mother on my first day at my important new job? I hit the ignore button and slide it back into my pocket, making a mental note to call her back later.

Then it's just me and the female writer left in the room, and I have no idea what I'm supposed to do next.

She smiles at me as she hangs her laptop bag over her shoulder. I smile back, still holding the empty tray.

"So," she says. "Did Malcolm give you something to do today? Or a writer to shadow?"

"Um, no," I say slowly. "Was he supposed to?"

She smiles like she feels sorry for me but doesn't answer my question. "It's okay! You can hang with me if you like. I can find plenty of things for you to do."

"Cool!" I lift my index and middle fingers to my temple and salute . . . because that's a thing I do now, I guess. "I am at your service."

She laughs, and we head out the door and down the hallway.

"I'm Jane," she says, reaching out to shake my hand. Her emerald green eyes sparkle behind dark lashes, and her brows are perfectly arched. She's probably the first person I've come across in LA who is even paler than I am. "I'm an EP—executive producer. I started as a staff writer on season one and worked my way up, so if you have any questions or need anything while you're here, I'm happy to help."

I beam at her. I've seen her name in the opening credits so many times. I'm so excited I could scream. But I don't want to freak her out, so I promise myself I'll stay chill.

That lasts about three seconds.

"You wrote the prom night episode last season, right?" I ask as we leave the building.

Her eyes widen like she's surprised I knew that, then a smile tugs at her lips. "I did."

I clutch my chest. "That was one of my favorite episodes ever! The moment Jonah finally admitted his feelings for Sue . . ." I dip my head back and swoon, "I cried."

Her smile reaches her eyes. "Oh, wow. I'm so happy you liked it!"

I keep bombarding her with questions about what it's like to work here, where else she's worked, and how she got into the business. She answers my questions with excited ramblings that I eat up. Jane talks to me like I'm a person, and for the first time today, I feel like I'm going to be okay here.

I'm so caught up in our conversation that I don't pay attention to where we're going until we reach a tall steel door.

"You've been watching since season one, I'm guessing?" Jane asks as she uses both arms to drag it open.

"Never missed an episode," I say, suddenly realizing where we are. I'm frozen still as the door slides open to reveal a sound-stage the size of an aircraft hangar. Noise filters out into the street where I'm standing, my jaw practically hitting the ground. People rush in every direction, some talking into their head-pieces, others moving equipment across the concrete floors. It's like opening a portal into a new world.

Jane walks ahead of me and I hurry to keep up. My head darts from left to right as I try to look at everything at once.

"Welcome to Silver Falls," she says.

I stare in awe at the sight before me. It's the exterior of the cabin that Jonah and Tom (played by Will and Archer) retreat to every full moon, in the woods just outside Silver Falls. I feel like I've stepped into my TV.

"Are you okay?" Jane asks with a laugh. I pull my jaw back off the ground and nod.

"I'm just so happy," I croak. I try to rein in my glee, reminding myself that I'm here to learn and work—I need to be professional. But I make a mental note to have a celebratory dance party the moment I get back to Parker's.

"Here," Jane says as she hands me a copy of the script for the episode being filmed. Her name is on the front.

"You wrote this episode?" I ask.

She nods. "I mean, it's all very collaborative. But yes."

I start flipping through the script and land on a page that says . . .

EXT. THE CABIN—NIGHT
Jonah, Tom, and Sasha are outside the
cabin. Fog swims around their ankles.
Jonah and Sasha are packing the truck to
leave Silver Falls. Tom watches from the
porch.

"This is the scene that's being set up?" I ask.

Jane glances at the page and nods. "It's only a few lines of dialogue, but we'll probably be here through lunch."

"I can't wait to see it all come together!"

"Good!" she says. "Why don't you take notes? Lines sometimes get tweaked or details changed, so I need someone to edit the script as we go."

I pull my pencil case out of my bag. "Sure thing."

Just then, Alyssa Huntington and Will Horowitz walk by, chatting about their lines. Alyssa is black, her body lean and athletic, with a contagious smile. She usually wears her hair shaved super short, but I notice it's grown out a little on top, with a cool fade on the sides. Her tattoos are mostly hidden under her clothes: a dark red leather jacket paired with skinny jeans and combat boots. Will is tall, maybe six feet, with light skin, wavy brown hair, and a permanent five-o'clock shadow that makes him look older than twenty-three. Parker is going to be so jealous that I'm breathing the same air as his crush.

I can't believe how close I am to my faves right now. Alyssa makes eye contact with me and I smile. She smiles back and it feels like time has slowed down. I stare after her as she takes a seat in a chair with her name on it, only a few feet away.

"Pretty cool to see all this, huh?" Jane asks me.

"The coolest," I say.

A young guy paces near us, talking into a walkie. "Does anyone have eyes on Archer? We need Archer!"

I hear a ton of footsteps walking through the soundstage and turn to see a small group of important-looking people walking toward the set. A woman with dark brown skin and very high heels seems to be the center of attention in the group.

"I'll be right back," Jane says as she hurries to talk to her.

As the entourage gets closer, I recognize the woman from a feature *Teen Vogue* did on her last year. Her name is Ruby Randall, and she's the first black woman to be named head of a major television network. She's the biggest boss around.

"Bex," Jane says, waving me over. "This is Ruby Randall, the head of the network. Ms. Randall, Bex is our new intern in the writers' room. It's her first day."

Ms. Randall smiles like I'm an old friend. "Hello! First day here and you're already on set. Glad to see you're diving right in!"

I shake her hand a little too enthusiastically, but she doesn't seem to mind.

"I'm having a blast!" I say. "Thank you for giving me such an amazing opportunity."

"I always say it's important for us to lift as we climb," she says. "I hope you learn a lot during your time here."

I gesture to the script in my hand. "I've already started taking notes."

She laughs. "A girl after my own heart."

Malcolm walks into the building then, with Dirk following him like a shadow.

"Looks like everything is running smoothly," Malcolm says. He turns to Dirk. "Dirk, Danish." Dirk scurries over to the craft services table and picks up a plate.

"Malcolm," Ms. Randall says. "It's great to see you giving your intern a real hands-on experience by inviting her to the set. I wish I'd had someone like that when I was a young intern." She looks at me, rolling her eyes. "All I did was fetch coffees for people who didn't even remember my name."

I'm about to say that it was Jane's idea to bring me to set, but Malcolm speaks first.

"Yes," he says. "Well, interns are the future, I always say."

Wow. I look at Jane, who's smiling and going along with it, so I follow her lead. This isn't like in high school, where I could just keep my head down, get my work done, and avoid eye contact with everyone else. I actually have to talk to people here, and be, like, social.

"That's great, Malcolm," Ms. Randall says. Her assistant arrives and beckons her away, and the moment she's out of sight, Malcolm leaves, too.

I watch Jane out of the corner of my eye, wondering if I should say something. The last thing I want to do is cause trouble on my first day, but I can't be the only one in this whole studio who notices Malcolm's behavior.

"I know what you're thinking," she says. I pretend to not know what she's talking about, but acting has never been a skill of mine. She smirks. "'Interns are the future, I always say,'" she says, lowering her voice and puffing her chest out to impersonate him. Then she rolls her eyes. "No one says that."

I chuckle but remind myself to be careful of what I say. "I don't think he likes me very much."

She frowns. "He doesn't like anyone very much. And trust me, the feeling is mutual. But he makes great television."

"Hey, Jane," a voice says from behind me. I turn around to see Archer Carlton walking toward us. My breath catches in my throat. "I have a few Qs for you to A about my lines," he says to Jane.

"Sure," Jane says. "What's up?"

He notices me standing next to her and looks me up and down. I grin at him like the huge *Silver Falls* fangirl that I am. He smiles. Oh my sweet lord. He's going to talk to me. Archer Carlton is going to speak words at me and I can't deal. This is a pivotal moment in my life. He opens his mouth to speak . . .

"I'll take a green juice, thanks."

Okay, so that's not exactly what I was hoping for, but this is part of my job now, so I drop everything to make his wish my command. Only I don't know where I'm supposed to find green juice in this place. Dirk is still at the craft table, so I go over to introduce myself and ask him.

"Hey!" I say with a friendly smile. "I didn't get a chance to introduce myself in the writers' room. I'm Bex, Malcolm's new intern."

He doesn't look up from the table as he piles Danishes onto a plate. "Don't talk to me."

For a second I think I misheard him, so I try again. "Do you know where I can find green juice? Archer wants some, and it's my first day so—"

"Do I look like a tour guide?" he asks. His phone dings in his pocket, but we both ignore it.

I shrink back a little. "No."

His phone dings again, but he ignores it again. "Listen, intern. There's a hierarchy you need to learn." He gestures with his hands, measuring the rankings. "It goes Randall, Malcolm, me, then literally everyone else in the whole fucking world, then right here at the bottom? That's you. You're a speck."

I want to crawl under the craft table and hide. I feel just like Andy in *The Devil Wears Prada*, naive, frazzled, and completely out of my depth. And Dirk just went full Emily on me.

"Sorry," I say. "I didn't mean to upset you. It's just that we both work for Malcolm, so I thought we could help each other out."

He raises an eyebrow. His phone dings three more times, and he groans while pulling it out of his pocket. "I'm so over this." He starts typing something, then glances up at me.

"Actually," he says. "There is something you could help me with."

I smile, feeling like he's coming around. "Sure!"

"Ms. Randall has asked a few select people to take over the

Silver Falls social accounts," he explains. "So fans can get a glimpse of what life on set is like. I've been running the Instagram, but it's so . . ." He pauses, like he's trying to find the words. "Superficial. And all these fangirls just won't stop with the comments and the questions and tagging me in their fanfic posts." He chuckles, then takes a step closer. "It's not for me. Someone like you, however, could be perfect for this role."

I smile, not really sure if he's being fake nice or real nice, but I want him to like me. And I don't want to be a speck. "I'd love to do that!"

"Great!" he says. "All you need to do is post some stories, photos, maybe a livestream or two. No spoilers, of course, but just enough content to keep the fans frothing for more."

He gives me the log-in details, and I'm genuinely excited to be taking on such an important responsibility. He may not understand the power of social media in the fandom, but I know from experience how important it is.

"Thank you," I say. "Now, seeing as we're helping each other, do you mind telling me where I can find green juice?"

He starts walking away. "I have no idea. Sorry!"

. . .

The rest of my day is spent running errands. Fetching an assorted variety of beverages, making phone calls, delivering paperwork, and making script notes for Jane on set. I even manage to snap a few photos for the *Silver Falls* Instagram and reply to some of the comments. As hectic as it sounds, I love every minute of it—at least the minutes when Malcolm and Dirk are out of sight.

It's dark by the time I leave. Hayley Kiyoko serenades me through my headphones as the bus rolls down the highway. My Ritalin wore off hours ago and it shows: I can barely keep my head up, I'm so tired.

I have a love/hate relationship with Ritalin. When I take it, it energizes me. I become very talkative and animated and focused. I get shit done. I'm awake. But there's an undercurrent of anxiety, a truly uncomfortable feeling in my chest, the kind you would get when you're running late to the most important meeting of your life. But if I don't take it? I'm half-asleep all day. I move like a sloth. I never know which task to focus on first, and if I do my focus never lasts long enough to see it to completion. There's no in-between with me—it's either sleepy sloth or Energizer Bunny. And right now I'm in peak sloth mode; even the jolting stop-and-start bus ride through Los Angeles can't keep me awake.

By the time I walk to Parker's from the bus stop, it's past nine. I fetch my key out of my bag and try to unlock the door, but once again it won't budge. Before I have time to test Parker's über-complicated trick, he opens the door, smiling.

"Finally!" he says as he pulls me into his arms. I relax into his hug, my cheek resting against his shoulder. "I've been waiting all day to give you this hug."

He leads me inside and closes the door. "I'm so proud of you. Now, tell me everything that you saw today, starting with Will Horowitz."

CHAPTER SIX

"Rise and shine!" Parker sings as he opens the blinds. The early-morning sunshine falls over me, and I hiss at him before rolling back over. I forgot that Parker is a morning person. His one flaw.

"Come on," he says. "If your butt isn't in the car by eight A.M., I'm leaving without you. I have a client to pretty up in Beverly Hills."

I groan into my pillow. "I just need ten more hours."

He cackles. "You and me both."

Parker disappears into the bathroom and I promptly fall back asleep. Ten minutes later, I'm woken up again by his panicked voice.

"Rebecca!" he says, sounding eerily like my mom when she's pissed at me. "We have to leave in, like, five minutes! Get your ass up!"

I groan again and drag myself off the futon and into the bathroom. I don't have time to shower, so I smother myself in deodorant and dry shampoo.

"Ready!" I say as I emerge from the bathroom in a cloud of Batiste. I go to the kitchen, pour myself a glass of orange juice, and swallow my Lexapro and Ritalin. Then Parker hands me my backpack and ushers me out the door.

The moment my butt hits the passenger seat, my nerves riot. I hoped I'd feel more confident about today, but it turns out second-day anxiety is even worse than first-day nerves. Suddenly, I feel like I'm on my way to Westmill High, knowing the assholes are waiting in the halls, not knowing what insults they'll hurl my way today.

But I have a plan: I'm going to swing by the café first, pick up coffees for all the writers (apparently the studio has an account there), and show up in time to hear the morning meeting.

An hour later, I arrive at room 121 with a tray full of coffees, and I get a hero's welcome.

"You're a lifesaver," Jane says as she cradles her cup like it's a delicate flower.

"Thanks, Bex," Andy says.

Even Malcolm had something not-rude to say. "Okay, intern. How fast are you at typing?"

"Um," I say. "Pretty fast, I guess."

He chuckles. "Good. Dirk is out picking up a pen I ordered. Again. You can take notes during the meeting. We get our best ideas from the conversations we have around this table, so it's important that someone records that."

"Done," I say. I sit down on the couch—which feels like a huge step up from being frozen in the corner yesterday—open my laptop, and start a new Word doc. I have to admit, I'm pretty proud of myself for being on top of things this morning. And Malcolm is actually giving me an important task. I think it's safe to say I've officially clocked the morning meetings! Next: world domination.

For the next hour, my fingers fly over the keyboard as they go over the episode together. Lines are rewritten. Scenes are swapped. Suggestions are made. I'm so enthralled that I never want this meeting to end.

Parker was right: This is what I want to do. I'm so glad he didn't let me run away from this.

Andy stands up and stares at the whiteboard, hands on hips. "We need to find a way to get from here"—he points to episode 611 on the board, the one we're working on now—"to one of the hunters turning into a wolf in the finale." He scratches his head. Everyone stares quietly at the board. Jane chews on the end of her pen, her eyes narrowed in thought.

"Alyssa is staying on for the rest of the season," she says. "It would be great for her to have a pivotal role in turning the hunter."

Malcolm nods. "The network does want her to stay as long as possible. She's bringing in great ratings."

I have an idea. It might be a shitty idea. They might hate it or think it's an amateur move. But I want to offer something to this meeting; I want to prove that I can speak up and be of use to this team. I take in a deep breath to prepare myself and straighten my shoulders.

"What if she has to turn the hunter in order to save them?" I suggest. My voice only shook a teeny bit, so I'm satisfied.

"I was thinking along those lines, too," Jane says. Phew. I smile at her, and she smiles back.

Andy nods, still standing in front of the board. "That could work."

It feels so good to be listened to. I sit up straighter, prouder.

"Interns are supposed to be quiet," Malcolm says. "Besides, that idea has been done. A superfan like you should know that, Becky."

Aaaand I'm back to Becky. My gaze drops to my keyboard.

"Everything's been done," Jane says. She says it with a smile, but her tone is stern. "But we can find a way to add a new spin to it."

"Who did I assign episode 612 to?" Malcolm asks, staring straight past Jane and at the board. Jane clenches her jaw. I can't believe she—a senior writer, an executive producer—is being straight-up ignored like this.

Everyone glances at one another. Andy clears his throat, then says, "Um, Mal, you were supposed to write 612, remember?"

The question seems innocent enough, but I swear Malcolm glares at Andy for a moment. Others at the table exchange looks that I don't understand. I feel like I'm missing an inside joke, only it's not funny, it's tense.

"Right," Malcolm says as he shifts in his chair. "I knew that." He looks at his watch and closes his laptop. "Okay, let's break for lunch."

I pack up my laptop as everyone starts to leave. I feel someone watching me, and when I look up Malcolm is glaring at me.

"Don't ever interrupt our meetings again."

I swallow hard. "Okay. Sorry."

"You completely threw me off track," he adds.

"Sorry," I say again. My heart sits in my stomach, like it's trying to hide.

Malcolm throws his stuff into his bag and storms out of the room. I fight back tears as I gather my things, feeling like all the progress I made this morning has just been washed away.

CHAPTER SEVEN

"Are you okay?" Jane asks in the hallway.

I put on a smile. "Yeah. Totally. I'm just gonna go to the bathroom. I'll meet you on set."

I'm overwhelmed and frustrated and need to take a minute alone. The second I lock the stall door, I feel relieved. My breathing slows. I let a tear or two fall down my cheeks.

I thought my days of eating lunch alone on a toilet were over the day I graduated. But every time I start to gain even just a little confidence in this place, it gets crushed all over again.

My phone buzzes and I find it at the bottom of my bag. My mom and Gabby have both texted me more than once to ask how I am. I leave Mom's unread, figuring I'll reply to it later. I don't want to tell her I'm hiding in the bathroom.

Gabby: ok I need you to tell me if you're dead or not because you never called to tell me what happened on your first day

Bex: I'm alive.

Gabby: having fun?!

Bex: that's a very complicated question

Gabby: uh oh. What happened?

Bex: I don't think I'm cut out for this life

Gabby: which life?

Bex: adult life. Those memes are right. Adulting is hard.

Gabby: Dude. It's only your second day!

Bex: don't remind me

Gabby: wtf happened.

Bex: Parts of it are amazing and I saw the set and the cast and I love so much of it. But my boss is a dick.

Gabby: Okay #1: everyone's boss is a dick. #2: YOU SAW THE SET AND THE CAST?! Hello!!!

Bex: yeah that was awesome

Gabby: do I need to come all the way down there and slap you until you realize how lucky you are?!

Bex: I said it was awesome!

Gabby: okay. what did the dick boss do?

Bex: he just embarrassed me in front of everyone. I suggested an idea for a story line and he was like "interns are supposed to be quiet, becky."

Gabby: wait who's becky?

Bex: I am

Gabby: you're not becky!

Bex: I KNOW I'M NOT BECKY

Gabby: I'm so confused. FT?

I dab my tears on some torn-off toilet paper, then call her on FaceTime.

"Hey," I whisper when she answers.

"Aww," she says. "Are you in the bathroom?"

"Yep," I say, popping my mouth on the *p*.

"Damn, Bex," she says. "You're a bit of a hot mess."

"This is what I'm saying."

She sighs into the phone. "You can't do this to yourself, babe. If you let people walk all over you, it's gonna be just like high school again. It's all new and scary, I get that. But you can't let everything get you down. You need to stand up for yourself."

"But he's my boss!" I say.

"Yeah," she says. "But that doesn't give him the right to embarrass you, or ignore you, or call you by the wrong name."

I shrug. "I could be Becky."

She glares at me through the phone. "No. You go back out there and tell him you are Bex Phillips and you will not be talked down to."

I roll my eyes. "Okay. Or I could just stop fooling myself and come back to Westmill." I say it as a joke . . . sort of.

"Hey!" she yells, making me jump. "Listen to me, dude. You have fought hard to be there. You have every right to be there. And you need to stand your ground on this. Don't give up."

A stray tear runs down my cheek, and I dab at it with the toilet paper. "Thanks, Gabs."

The door to the bathroom creaks open, and I hurry to end the call.

"Sorry, gotta go," I whisper. "I'll text you later, bye."

I end the call and throw the phone back into my bag like it's about to explode. Then I drop my head into my hands and close my eyes. I could really use a nap right now. But instead, I leave the stall and stand over the sink to splash my face.

"I'm Bex Phillips," I whisper to myself. "And I will not be talked down to."

I say it again. And again. Then once more. Each time I repeat it, I feel stronger, bolder, prouder.

I just hope Malcolm takes it as well as the bathroom mirror is. I dab my puffy eyes with a paper towel, straighten the collar of my shirt, then march out the door.

"I'm Bex Phillips, dammit," I say as I walk down the hall to Malcolm's office. "My name isn't Becky. Or 'doll.' Or 'intern.' It's Bex fucking Phillips."

By the time I reach his door I'm so riled up, I could burst

through it like the Kool-Aid guy. I knock on the door, repeating my name over and over again in my mind.

"Hey, Bex," a voice says from behind me. I turn to see Jane leaving her office. "Whatcha doin'?"

"I just need to talk to Malcolm," I say, then knock again.

"Oh," she says. "He's gone for the day. Probably to work on the script for 612."

Fuckity.

She must see the disappointment on my face, because she frowns. "Is there anything I can help you with?"

I shake my head. All the boldness I had running through my veins starts to fade.

"Come on," she says. "Let's head to the set. We're filming a fun new scene today."

Just like that, I perk up again. Spending a whole day in Silver Falls is exactly what I need right now. At least there I can be useful. And I get to hang out with actors and directors and help make Jane's script come to life.

"For what it's worth," Jane says as we walk through the lot, "I thought you had great input this morning. Don't give up."

My heart grows twice its size. "Thank you."

"Don't mention it," she adds. "This is a hard business. There's a lot of rejection, and I don't want you to let that get you down. Sometimes you need to fight to be heard, especially when you're the only woman in a room full of men."

Her words echo in my mind. *Sometimes you need to fight to*

be heard. But I'm not a fighter. In fact, all evidence points to the exact opposite. When faced with confrontation, I crumble. I cower. I cry. How am I supposed to fight to be heard if my voice buries itself in my chest like a startled rabbit whenever I need it? Hell, one of the reasons I started writing was to release everything I'd ever wanted to say out loud but couldn't.

Wait. That's it. I'll fight to be heard using the most valuable weapon I have in my arsenal: writing.

I'm going to write a killer script for episode 612. If I can't tell Malcolm who I am, I'm going to show him. I'm going to make sure he remembers my name.

When we get to set, I start writing down ideas on my phone in between taking scene notes for Jane and fetching green juices for Archer. The only thing I'm sure of for the episode is this: The hunter will be a girl. She will be queer. And she and Alyssa's character, Sasha, will fall in love.

CHAPTER EIGHT

EXT. SILVER FALLS WOODS—NIGHT

We open on Sasha's boots as she
runs through the woods. The sound of
motorbikes echoes in the distance. The
hunters are on her tail. The camera pans
out to show Jonah, Sasha, and Tom
running together. They're sweaty, dirty,
out of breath.

                  MALE HUNTER

(Offscreen)

    We're comin' for you, dogs!

Jonah trips and falls. Tom keeps
running, but Sasha stops to help him up.

                    SASHA

        Get up!

                    TOM

        (Breathing heavily)
        We can't outrun them like this. We
        have to turn.

                    SASHA

        So let's turn.

They both transform into their wolf
selves, then keep running through the
woods. A shot fires from behind, hitting
a tree ahead. Branches fall in front of
Sasha, blocking her path and separating
her from the others. She runs around it
but gets caught in a net. She tries
chewing her way through it, but it's
electrified. A bike skids to a stop
nearby. Boots hit the ground as one of
the hunters slowly approaches the net.
The hunter stands in the light of the
moon and takes her helmet off, revealing
her identity as Lyla. Sasha growls,
baring her teeth.

Lyla crouches in front of the net. Sasha
growls more but stops when she cuts her
free.

                    LYLA

        Go. Hurry.

Sasha runs. Lyla watches her.

END TEASER.

I look up from my laptop just as the bus pulls up to my stop. I throw it into my bag and jump up from my seat just in time. My mind races as I speed-walk to Parker's building. Scenes play on a projector screen in my mind. Lines of dialogue repeat over and over. I can't wait to write the moment Sasha and the hunter meet again. I know Parker's home, so I knock instead of wrestling with the door again. There's no time for that when I'm on such a roll.

"Hey, girl!" he says with a smile. He's wearing an apron over jeans and a T-shirt that says LET BOYS BE FEMININE. "I made pasta! That's dinner sorted for the week."

The whole apartment smells like vodka sauce. My stomach rumbles. "Great, thank you! I'll eat while I work."

"Oooh!" he says, raising an eyebrow. "A project! Is it top secret?"

I sit cross-legged on the couch and set up my laptop again. "Um, kinda? As in, no one really knows I'm doing it. My boss is a disrespectful jerk, so I'm writing a killer episode to prove him wrong about me."

"A spite script," he says as he stirs the pasta. "I love it."

"Thanks! So, how was your day?"

He fixes a plate for me and leaves it on the counter. "Hectic. I did a charity fashion show in Beverly Hills. So many pretty people there."

Parker's phone alarm goes off on the coffee table, and he lights up. "That's my cue! Wish me luck!

"You're going out?" I ask, confused.

He unties his apron and swings it around his neck like it's a cape, then stands in a superhero pose with his hands on his hips. "I have a date!"

I close my laptop. "A date? Since when?"

"Since this morning," he says. "I met a very cute model at the fashion show. His name is Dante, and we flirted a little while I did his makeup. Anywho, he asked me out for drinks at Bar 161."

I clap my hands. "Yay! That's so exciting!"

He hangs the apron on the magnet hook on the fridge, and

I notice his fingers trembling. "I've never been so nervous about a boy before. He's just so pretty."

"Hey," I say, standing up from the couch. "You're just as pretty as any model." I'm not lying; Parker has magnificent blue eyes and perfectly arched brows, and he isn't afraid to rock a bit of highlighter.

"Oh, I know," he says, flipping his head back like he has long, luscious locks. "But Dante . . . ," he swoons.

"Okay," I say. "I need to see a pic of this dude, obviously."

He picks up his phone and googles him. Dozens of professional photos appear on the screen. Dante Smith is his name, and good lord is he pretty. He has dark brown skin, dreads in a topknot with a fade, a dazzling smile, and striking hazel eyes. Parker taps on a black-and-white shirtless photo, with Dante posing casually against a raindrop-adorned window.

"Holy fuck," I say.

"This is what I'm saying," Parker says, swooning again.

"He has a six-pack," I say.

Parker closes the screen and fans himself with his hand. "Stop! I'm nervous enough already."

I place a hand on his shoulder. "P. You'll be fine. Now go, or you'll be late."

He grabs his keys and his wallet and opens the door, then turns to me. "You'll be okay here?"

I nod. "I've got a script to write."

. . .

"ILY" by the Brightsiders is blasting through my headphones when the front door is kicked open at 2:00 A.M. Parker waltzes in, smiling like he's either drunk or in love—or both.

"You're still awake!" he says, then shushes himself for being too loud. Yep, definitely drunk. "How much Ritalin have you had?"

"Don't worry," I say. "I've had the recommended daily amount. I'm just in the zone."

I have to keep going. It's just the way my mind works. There's no way I'll be able to sleep or shower or even think of anything else until this is finished. It would crawl under my skin and eat away at me. "How was your date?"

His grin gets even wider, then he closes the door and leans against it, sighing. "Heavenly." He peels himself away from the door and sashays into the kitchen, humming to himself. "We talked, we drank, we danced, we made out like the world was ending."

I giggle, getting high off his lovestruck fumes. He takes some leftover chocolate cake out of the fridge and starts digging into it like a zombie into guts.

"He invited me to a pool party on Saturday," he says before popping some into his mouth. "It's at his friend Chloe's place. As in Mix Chloe, the singer."

I move my laptop off me and stand up. "Wait. Mix Chloe?!

I love them! I was just listening to their song with the Bright-siders!"

Chloe is a black nonbinary femme YouTuber and musician. I've been watching their videos since middle school.

"You wanna come with?" he asks. "Dante said I could bring friends."

I gasp. "Fuck yes!"

Parker claps excitedly, sending cake crumbs flying all over the kitchen from his fingers. "Oops."

"Okay," I say, taking the massacred cake plate away from him. "I think it's time for bed. We both have work in the morning."

Parker gives me a crooked smile. "Okeydokey, Loki."

. . .

On Friday morning, I walk into the writers' room with my usual tray of coffees and my finished script in my bag. I've had a total of five hours sleep since Wednesday, but I have enough adrenaline and Ritalin in me to last the day. I hope.

Everyone sits around the table. Dirk is ready to take notes on his laptop, and I sit in an empty chair in the corner of the room to listen quietly.

"Mal," Jane says just before we wrap up. "Can you update us on episode 612? Just so we all know what we're doing."

He's been oddly MIA the last couple of days, and when he

has shown up, he's been very quiet. Puffy bags sit under his eyes, salt-and-pepper stubble lines his jaw, and his hair is a mess. He looks like he hasn't slept in months.

"It's fine," he says. "It'll be ready to table at Monday's meeting."

"Great!" Jane says. "Can't wait to see how you introduced the new hunter."

"Well," he says, sounding kind of annoyed. "Like I just said, you'll find out on Monday." He stands up and leaves then, and all the writers exchange looks. But once again, no one says anything.

I really want to give Malcolm my script before he leaves, so I hurry out of the room and chase him down the hall.

"Mr. Butler!" I call. His head turns slightly, but he keeps walking. "Can I talk to you for a sec?"

He sighs and turns around. "Whatever it is, ask Dirk."

"It's important," I say as I hold my script out to him. "I wrote my own version of episode 612." My heart is beating so hard I feel like I can hear it in my voice. "Just to show you what I can do."

He looks at me like I've asked him for a kidney. "Look, Becky, you've been here, what, five days? So I guess I can let your naivety slide just this once. I have an entire production to run here; do you think I have time to read the work of an intern? Dirk has been my writing assistant for a year and he's never asked me to read a spec."

My heart drops into my stomach. I'm so embarrassed. Instead of proving my initiative to him, all I've done is show him how ignorant I am about how things work here.

"I'm so sorry," I say, not even able to look at him. I turn to walk away.

"Wait," he says. "Did you say you wrote a spec for 612?"

I nod. "I know you've already written it, but—"

"Right, yeah," he says. Then he takes a step closer, his gaze on the script in my hands. "Can I see it?"

My eyebrows shoot up, and he gives me a small smile. I hand it to him and wait with bated breath as he flips through it.

"Hmm." He looks up and down the hall, which is empty besides the two of us, then closes the script and tucks it under his arm. "Listen, I'm not promising anything. But if I have time over the weekend, I'll take a look at it."

I'm so happy I could do a backflip, but I keep my composure. "Thank you so much, Malcolm. Wow."

He shrugs. "I can be nice when I want to be. Just don't tell Dirk about this, okay?"

I slide my index finger and thumb over my lips in the zipping motion. "Deal."

Then he turns and walks away, leaving me standing there, stunned. A big part of me never thought he would actually take it, but I guess Jane was right: Sometimes you have to fight to be heard.

CHAPTER NINE

Parker walks into Chloe's party like he's strutting down a catwalk. I push my glasses higher up on my nose, trailing behind him like his shadow. I figure if I stay close to him, no one will realize I don't really belong here.

Loud pop music bounces off the cool gray walls, making hips swing and voices sing. Drinks are flowing, famous faces are mingling, and here I am, a closeted intern from Westmill. I feel so out of place, and yet there's a secret part of me that knows this is where I'm meant to be. So I'm going to try to act like it.

"Dante should be here somewhere," P says to me. I nod and look around while twisting one of the buttons on my shirt.

I didn't like any of my clothes this morning, so Parker let me wear one of his shirts that I've been lusting after since I got to LA. It's a white button-down with an adorable pug print all over it. It's masculine and quirky and I love it. And for some reason that I haven't quite figured out yet, wearing Parker's shirt makes me stand a little taller. I may not be totally comfortable at this party, but I'm feeling comfortable in my skin. I matched it with my old skinny jeans that have holes in the knees from being worn so often—they're my only pair. Thank the fashion gods that ripped jeans are on trend right now. I can't wait until I have money so I can start buying clothes that actually feel like *me*, but for now I'm happy to raid P's wardrobe as long as he lets me.

"There he is," Parker says in my ear. I follow his gaze across the crowded room. Dante is sitting on the arm of a couch, wearing geek glasses, a white tee, and ripped jeans. A gold bow holds his dreads together on top of his head. He spots us through the sea of celebrities and flashes his pearly whites. Then he stands up and moves through the party effortlessly, his gaze on Parker. I feel Parker stop breathing next to me.

"Hey, boy," Dante says when he reaches us. Then he kisses Parker on the cheek, and it's all so sweet I could die.

"Well, hello," P says, then immediately forgets I exist. They start talking quietly, whispering sweet nothings to each other. I start edging away, trying to give them some space, but I don't know where to go.

In an effort to be more outgoing, I try to make eye contact with a pretty girl sitting on the kitchen island. She looks over to me, a smile growing on her dark red lips, and I perk up instantly. I'm about to walk closer, when someone pushes past me. It's a dude in a loose-fitting orange tank top tucked into skinny jeans, and he steps right up to the pretty girl and lifts her off the counter in a bear hug.

Oh. She wasn't smiling at me. She was smiling at orange tank top dude. I back away, my gaze darting around to make sure nobody saw that embarrassing moment. Then I wander aimlessly through the party, taking everything in. Chloe's house is stunning, with high ceilings, walls of shelves adorned with vintage records, music awards, and books, and a huge framed photograph of Prince above the fireplace.

"Yo!" a voice says. It sounds familiar, but no one knows me here, so I ignore it. Someone taps me on the shoulder. "Hey! Green juice girl!" I turn around to see Archer Carlton smiling at me. "I knew it was you!"

"Oh, hey!" I say. "I'm Bex, by the way. Not . . . not green juice girl."

He laughs. "Cool, right. I didn't know you knew Chloe."

"I don't," I say. "My cousin is here with Dante Smith, so . . ."

"Nice," he says, nodding. "You're an intern, right? How's that going?"

I can't wipe the grin from my face. I'm actually talking to Archer Carlton at Mix Chloe's party. If only the kids from school could see me now.

"I'm loving it," I say, smiling. "I'm learning so much already. And being on set is a dream."

He chuckles, then takes a swig of his beer. "Well, I appreciate all the green juices. I wanted to talk to you more on set, but I just get really involved in the work. Not, like, Daniel Day-Lewis involved, but I really have to focus, you know?"

I nod, still in awe that this is really happening. "That's totally fair. I wasn't, like, offended or anything."

He sighs, like he's relieved. "Thank god. I worry that I come off as a real dick sometimes."

I chuckle. "I don't think you're a—"

Before I can finish reassuring him that he's not a dick, he steamrolls into a story.

"Like, this one time," he says, his voice louder than before, like he's talking to an audience and not just me. "I was in the green room at *Jimmy Fallon* with Rebel Wilson and Idris Elba, and I made this joke . . ."

A circle of four or five people start to form around him as he continues. Someone edges in front of me, and I find myself at the back of a growing crowd, all listening to him like he's a prophet.

"Speaking of Jimmy Fallon," he continues. "He begged me to tell this story on the show, but I wanted to keep it hush-hush. I was *this close*"—he pinches his thumb and index finger together—"to landing the role of Thor for the Marvel franchise." Some people gasp; my eyebrows shoot up toward my hairline.

"Right?" he says, leaning his elbow on the surface of the white grand piano behind him. "Me and Chris Hemsworth were waiting in the hall to audition. Poor guy was shaking, he was that nervous. I actually felt bad for the guy. Luckily for him, I had some relaxation techniques up my sleeve—my Zen master taught me all about that shit—and I helped calm him down. In hindsight, I probably should've just let him freak out. Maybe I would've been running around with that sick hammer instead of him! That's what I get for being a decent dude."

Everyone laughs, and more people squeeze in front of me. I try to stay close to hear more of his anecdotes, but his audience is so large now that I'm too far away to catch all of it.

It's kind of bizarre, seeing him this way. Monologing like he's performing Shakespeare, dropping famous names left and right. This is not how I pictured him at all.

In the show, Archer's character, Tom, is known for his one-liners. He's tight-lipped and brooding, the mysterious bad boy who walks into a bar and has beautiful girls with ample cleavage fall into his lap with just one smoldering eyebrow raise. It's not necessarily a bad thing that Archer's so vastly different from his character, but I can't help but feel uncomfortable with it. I had this image of him in my mind, and cracks are forming in that image right in front of my eyes. It's an odd thing to realize the person you've seen onscreen and in magazines for years is separate from the reality of who they are.

"Bex!" Parker calls, snapping me out of my thoughts. I turn around to see him and Dante walking over, hand in hand. "Where'd you go?"

I'm about to answer him when he notices Archer and completely flips out. "Oh my God! Archer fucking Carlton!"

He drags Dante closer to Archer, grinning from ear to ear.

A furry little creature wanders past, catching my eye. "A dog!" I gasp, then follow its wagging tail outside. It's a French bulldog, and it leads me to the edge of the yard, to a glass fence overlooking all of Los Angeles. I crouch down and pet it lightly on the head, then it comes closer and nuzzles up to me, officially making me feel like the coolest person at the party. New goal: make this pup my best friend before I leave.

"What's your name, little dude?" I lift the gold name tag on the bedazzled pink collar and giggle when I see it. "Bowie! Hello, Bowie, how are you, bud?" He responds by trying to lick my face, and I play with his velvet ears. Out of nowhere, two other dogs waddle over, a corgi named Freddie and a Dalmatian puppy named Jagger.

All three of them compete for my attention, climbing on me until I fall back onto my butt and give in to their cuteness. This is the best day ever.

"Well, you've found the best part of the party," a voice says.

"Right?" I reply, even though I can't see who's talking to me. "I couldn't resist their squishy faces."

I peek around the corgi butt in my face. It's Shrupty Padwal, Instagram star and YouTube celebrity. She went viral last year when she and Chloe posted a video of them singing about some of the racist, homophobic, transphobic, all-around-trash trolls they get. Like a musical version of reading mean tweets. But she found fame through makeup tutorials, skincare tips, and beauty product reviews for those with dark skin like hers.

Shrupty puts her drink on a nearby table, then sits cross-legged across from me. The puppies immediately attack her with kisses, leaving me high and dry. But I'm not mad; I'd choose her, too. She's beautiful, with her brown skin, long dark hair, and thick lashes. She's wearing green high-waisted shorts, a white Sailor Moon T-shirt, and gold aviator sunglasses pushed into her hair.

"Are you Archer's girl?" she asks me as Jagger climbs into her lap.

I point to myself. "Me? Nah." Should I say I'm gay? She's gay, so she'd be cool about it. My skin prickles at the thought of telling her, though. What if she doesn't believe me? Dammit. I really should've practiced in the mirror or something until I felt confident saying it.

"Oh," she says. "I saw you talking to him earlier, so I thought . . ." She shrugs and trails off.

"I work with him, kind of," I say. Have I missed my chance to tell her I'm gay? Am I supposed to just blurt it out randomly? Is that a thing gay people do? I've never met any other out queer people except for P. Ugh. *How do I gay?*

"You work on *Silver Falls*?" she asks. "Are you an actress?"

Just then, Bowie leaps onto me, his tail going wild. "I wish I could act," I say, laughing. "I'm an intern."

"I love that show," she says. "What's it like working there?"

I start telling her about my first week, how the cast are all so nice, how Jane has taken me under her wing, and how I gave Malcolm my script.

A light bulb sparks in my head. "Actually," I say. "You'd be my dream casting for the character I created."

She tilts her head to the side. "Really? You think?"

"Yeah!" The more I look at her, the more I see her owning that role. "You would rock it. I mean, think about it, a badass huntress, rides a motorbike, secretly saves wolves from being hunted down . . . then falls in love with Sasha."

She smiles. "That would be pretty fucking cool. I've been wanting to get into acting."

"You totally should," I say. "I mean, my script won't make it to air, it's just a spec. I'll be surprised if Malcolm actually reads it. But you'd be great in any role on *Silver Falls*."

She sweeps some of her hair behind her ear shyly. "Thanks."

"Shrupty!" a blond girl calls from across the pool. "Come on!" She taps on her wrist, like she's wearing a watch.

"Ah, shit," Shrupty says. "I gotta go. But, um . . ." She pauses, then flips her sunglasses over her eyes. "Can I get your number? You know, for networking purposes."

"Sure." I bite the insides of my cheeks as I give her my number, trying to suppress the wild grin that wants to take over my whole face.

She says good-bye, and I watch her as she walks away, with

the dogs following like they've imprinted on her. And now I'm sitting alone in the corner of the yard like the antisocial dork that I am, but I don't even care because Shrupty freaking Padwal just asked me for my number. Maybe her gaydar alerted her to me. Maybe she thinks I'm cute. Or maybe she just wants to be on *Silver Falls*.

My phone buzzes in my hand.

Shrupty: nice meeting you xo

CHAPTER TEN

Malcolm is late to the writers' room on Monday. He walks in carrying a stack of papers and a surprisingly friendly smile on his face. His hair is brushed, his eyes are clear, and he shaved. I hope that means he's in a good mood; I want to ask him if he had a chance to read my episode.

But I get my answer when he starts handing out the scripts. I flip open to the first page to see a very familiar scene.

EXT. SILVER FALLS WOODS—NIGHT
Jonah, Tom, and Sasha run through the woods. Hunters are close behind on dirt bikes.

          JONAH
We're almost there!

Sasha's leg gets stuck in a log. Jonah
and Tom keep running.

                    SASHA
        I'm stuck!

She has to turn to break free. She
transforms into a wolf, then keeps
running—straight into a trap. Before she
can fight her way out of it, one of the
hunters pulls up. It's a woman hunter,
Lyla, her black jumpsuit zipped down
just enough to reveal some cleavage. She
takes her helmet off, letting her long,
shiny hair fall past her shoulders.
Sasha growls at her.

                    LYLA
        Hush, wolfie. I'm Lyla, and I won't
        bite if you don't.

She cuts Sasha free.

                    LYLA
        Run.

```
Sasha races away. Lyla smiles, then
jumps back on her bike and rides away.


END TEASER.
```

I can't breathe. The script falls closed on my lap. His name is on the front, in all caps.

WRITTEN BY MALCOLM BUTLER

It's my script. This is my episode. I look up at Malcolm, sitting at the head of the table, reading over the episode with a proud smirk. The other writers at the table read it over, too, all of them nodding approvingly.

"Wow," Jane says, like she's impressed. "So, to be clear, Lyla is Sasha's new love interest?"

Malcolm leans back in his chair. "Yep."

"Nice," Andy says. "Viewers are going to eat this up."

"I figured it's time to give the gays what they want," Malcolm says with a dry laugh.

What the fuck. No. I'm the one giving the gays what they want! And he can't say "the gays"! Only gays like me can say that. Fuck. There are so many things going wrong right now, I don't know where to start. My skin runs hot from anger, and I break out into a sweat. Conflicting thoughts race through my mind.

He stole my script.

But it's not exactly the same.

I should say something.

No one's going to believe me.

I deserve some credit for this, at least.

Writing TV is a collaborative process; maybe this happens all the time.

He's trying to pass it off as his original work.

And he's the showrunner, so there's nothing I can do.

As the debate goes round and round in my head, the table has already started discussing the episode. So I do what I always do: listen and take notes. But my blood is quietly boiling.

. . .

By the time the meeting wraps up, I'm ready to explode. I don't know what to do. It would be so much easier to just let this go, and the thought of confronting him about it makes me nauseous. But I can't just let him steal my script. Can I?

I leave the building to get some air and text my voice of reason, Gabby.

Bex: remember the script I've been working on? The one I gave to my boss?

Gabby: yeah! Omg did he love it?

Bex: I guess so. He stole it.

Gabby: WHAT

Gabby: GTFO

Bex: he came into the meeting this morning with a rewritten version with his name on it

Gabby: omg bex I'm so sorry. Did you say anything?

Bex: no! I was too shocked.

Gabby: are you going to confront him?

Bex: idk.

Gabby: dude, you have to do something

Bex: what do I do??? HELP ME.

Gabby: ok stay calm and ask him about it. Maybe he just forgot to credit you?

Bex: unlikely.

Gabby: I know he totally stole it. But approach him about in a way that isn't accusatory. Then when he admits it you can demand he credits you.

Bex: I'm scared gabs

Gabby: I know. But you can handle this. It's just like when Emily kept stealing your Ritalin. You called her out and she stopped.

Oh god. Emily Rose was my mortal enemy all through high school. She'd terrorize me by following me through the halls, kicking my heels and muttering insults to her friends just loud enough for me to hear. Last year, I kept noticing some of my Ritalin was missing. I thought I was imagining things until I caught her with her head in my locker and her fingers in my prescription bottle.

But she didn't stop because I called her out; she stopped because I snitched to the principal and they made her take a drug test. Emily was one step ahead and took some pill that flushed her clean, so my Ritalin didn't show up on her results. I came to school to find her test results superglued to my locker, with the word LIAR written over it.

What if the same thing happens with Malcolm? What if

he twists it around just like Emily and makes me look like the bad guy?

He could ruin me. I'd never be able to get a job in television.

Gabby: Bex? What are you going to do?

Bex: nothing. I can't do anything. I need this job too much.

Five minutes later, I'm headed back to the writers' room to collect my laptop and meet Jane on set. But as I walk past Malcolm's office, I see him in the corner of my eye and get so overwhelmed by anger that I approach him.

"Mr. Butler," I say as I walk in and close the door. "I want to talk to you about episode 612."

He looks up at me from behind his desk. "I thought you might."

I have to admit, I'm taken aback by how open he's being about this. It's as though he does this all the time.

"You're not denying it?" I ask.

He shrugs. "Denying what?"

"You . . ." I pause, gather myself, and try again. "You stole my script."

Malcolm laughs. "Is that really how you see it?"

"That's not how I see it," I say. "That's how it *is*."

"Is it, though?" He flips the script open in front of me, the pages blowing air in my face. "Point to the lines that are yours. I'll wait."

He knows I can't. He's changed them all enough that I can't claim any of it. Except Lyla. "The hunter. Lyla. She's my character. She was my idea."

"Listen, Becky," he says with a smirk. "You're lucky I even read your script. If you remember, I didn't want it to begin with. But I decided to be a nice guy and help you out." He drops the script onto his desk. "You should be thanking me. What you wrote read like bad fanfiction. I turned it into something good. Something that actually deserves airtime."

I swallow the lump in my throat. "You wouldn't have an episode if it wasn't for me. You wouldn't have Lyla."

"You're blowing this way out of proportion." He opens up his laptop and mutters, "This is why women aren't cut out for this business. Too much drama."

My hands form fists at my sides. I'm too angry to even speak. He stares up at me, and I stare right back.

"Fine," he says with a sigh. "How about this?" He pulls the script toward himself, then takes a pen from his desk and starts writing on the cover page. "I'll give you a writing credit on this episode, if you let this go." He slides the script over to me. Under his printed name, he's scrawled "and Becky."

"My name," I say through gritted teeth, "is Bex Phillips."

He waves a hand dismissively. "Yeah, I'll have Dirk print it up like that. But do we have a deal?"

What choice do I have? He's going to use the script no matter what I say. And it's his word against mine. At least this way, I can take credit for Lyla. Then I think of Shrupty and add a final request.

"I won't tell anyone you stole my script," I say, my voice shaking. "If you give me a writing credit *and* let me have input in who gets cast to play Lyla."

He laughs like I made a joke. I use all my courage to keep staring him down. Then, realizing I'm dead serious, he taps his pen on the desk and nods slowly. "You never give up, do you?"

I turn my nose up at him. "No. I don't."

"Deal," he says.

"Deal."

He smiles. "Good. I'm glad we finally understand each other."

The moment I leave his office, I text Shrupty.

Bex: hey, remember that Silver Falls role I mentioned?

Shrupty: hey! yeah?

Bex: it just opened up!

Shrupty: wait what

Bex: You still interested?

Shrupty: hell yeah!

Bex: awesome! I'll send you the info.

CHAPTER ELEVEN

"She's not right for the role," Malcolm says. We just saw the tenth actress audition for the part of Lyla today. He's hardly even paid attention to any of them, instead spending the whole time texting. Luckily, Jane and Janice, the casting director, are here to make all the decisions. And they aren't so ready to dismiss actress number ten.

"Why's that?" Jane asks.

He keeps his attention on his phone. "Not enough . . ." He cups his palms in front of his chest, and I realize he's referring to the actress's breasts. I scoff quietly to myself. Janice glares at him, and Jane rolls her eyes. I think of Shrupty and how she's about to sit here before him and be judged by him. I should have warned her about him earlier.

Dirk enters the room, gesturing behind him. "This is Shrupty Padwal."

My heart perks up when I hear her name, taking me by

surprise. I've been waiting to see her walk through those doors all day. Thanks to my tip, she sent in her audition tape and made it through to today's audition round. But with Malcolm shrugging at every single actress we've seen, I'm starting to wonder if we'll have a Lyla by the end of the day like Janice hoped.

Just then, Shrupty walks in, her dark hair swept over to one side, a bright smile on her face, and I'm melting into my chair like a Popsicle on a hot summer day. She adjusts the collar of her gray blazer, which she's paired with a black V-neck blouse and cropped jeans.

"Thank you," she says to Dirk.

"My pleasure," he says while staring directly at her cleavage. "Again, I'm a big fan."

Shrupty clears her throat. "Do I have something on my shirt?"

Taken aback, Dirk immediately looks away. "No, no."

"Really?" she asks in a sarcastic tone. "Because you were really fixated just now."

My eyes dart back and forth between them like I'm watching a boxing match.

"Sorry," Dirk sputters, his face turning pink in panic. "I wasn't—"

Shrupty seems to burn a hole in him with her eyes as he tries to come up with an explanation for his gawking.

"Dirk," Malcolm interrupts. "That'll be all." And in a flash, Dirk has left the room.

Shrupty turns to us and smiles.

"Hi," she says as she approaches the desk and shakes our hands. When she takes my hand in hers, I feel a spark run from my fingers all through my body. My cheeks flush and I look down, trying to focus on my work, but she's in my head and I can't shake her.

"Let's begin," Jane says.

"I'll be her scene partner," I say. Jane gestures for me to take a seat opposite Shrupty, who gives me a grateful smile.

"Whenever you're ready," Janice says, watching her over her reading glasses.

Shrupty looks down at her script, clears her throat, then begins.

"If I wanted to kill you," she says, her voice low and serious, "you'd be dead already. I don't kill wolves."

I read Alyssa's part, Sasha. "So why ride with hunters?"

"They're all I have. They took me in after wolves killed my parents. But I'm not like them. I don't want to kill anymore."

"So you *have* killed wolves before?"

"Have you killed hunters before?"

"Only the ones who tried to kill me first."

"Okay, great," Janice says. "Let's move on to the next scene. Bex, you continue reading as Sasha, and I'll read Archer's part, Tom."

I flip a few pages ahead, to the scene where Lyla runs to warn Sasha, Tom, and Jonah that the hunters are coming.

Shrupty nods and takes in a deep breath.

"You need to go," she says, panting like she's been running. "My family knows you're here. They're coming."

"Who the hell are you?" Janice asks, reading as Tom.

"It doesn't matter," Shrupty says. "All that matters is that you're in danger. You need to leave. Now."

"How did they find us?" I ask.

Shrupty reaches out and touches my hand lovingly. "They followed me last night. They saw us together. Sasha, I'm so sorry."

"She's a hunter?" Janice asks angrily.

"She's not like them," I say. "She saved me." I turn to Shrupty. "Come with us."

"I can't," she says, shaking her head slowly. "I'll hold them off as long as I can, but you have to go. Run! Now!" Tears well up in her eyes, and I'm so mesmerized by her that I forget it's my line.

"Oh," I say, trying to find my place on the page. "Crap. Sorry."

"It's okay," Janice says. "Let's just do one more. Scene eleven. I'll read for Sherry, Lyla's adoptive mother."

I sit back in my chair, watching Shrupty as she disappears into the emotions of the scene.

"You lied to me," she says. "You told me my parents were murdered by wolves."

"They were murdered," Janice says.

Shrupty raises her voice. "By you! You hunted them down

like you always do. They were wolves, and they were good. I know the truth now, so don't you dare lie to me."

"I'm so sorry," Janice says. "I wanted to tell you. All I ever wanted to do was protect you."

"Protect me? Nothing you've ever done has been for me."

In the script, Lyla walks to the door, then turns back to look at her adoptive mother one last time.

"I always knew my parents were slaughtered by a monster," Shrupty says, choking back tears. "But I never in a million years thought *you* could be the monster."

The room falls silent for a moment, then Janice and Jane talk quietly to each other. I just stare at Shrupty, blown away. Even Malcolm looks impressed.

"Great," Janice says. "We can finish there."

"Thank you, Shrupty," Jane says, smiling. "That was really good."

Shrupty blinks away her tears and smiles. "Really? Thank you!"

"So good," I say. "Amazing."

She tucks her hair behind her ear and looks away, like she's embarrassed. "Thanks."

We all look at Malcolm, waiting for a response, but he just nods.

"Thank you so much for coming in," Janice says as she gives Shrupty a friendly smile and a handshake. "We'll let you know by the end of the day."

Shrupty leaves, and I wait with bated breath to hear the verdict.

"Well," Jane says, scribbling in her script. "I don't know where you found her, Bex, but she was really good. What do you think, Mal?"

He glances up at her. "She's pretty, she can act, and I have a dinner meeting to run to, so let's call it and get the hell out of here."

Janice claps her hands together. "Well then, I think we've found our Lyla."

I fist pump the air triumphantly. "For real? Can I go tell her the good news before she leaves?"

"Go ahead," Janice says.

My phone is in the writers' room, so I can't text or call Shrupty to come back. I have to hurry to catch up with her. I speed-walk out of the building just as she's driving away from the visitors' parking lot, but I'm too far away for her to see me waving at her. Maybe I can beat her to the exit.

I race through the back lot with a great big grin on my face, swerving past a group of extras in fifties-style poodle skirts and dodging an animatronic velociraptor being transported to a soundstage. A tour bus blocks my path to the main gate, so I have to take a shortcut through New York Street. Finally, I make it to the gate just as Shrupty is pulling up to the security window.

"Wait," I shout as I run in front of the car.

Shrupty lifts her sunglasses up, her eyes wide. "Bex! What the hell, girl?"

I'm so excited, I don't care how ridiculous I look. I drum my hands on the hood of her car. "You got it!"

Shrupty rolls her window down and sticks her head out. "What?"

"You got the part!" I yell. "You're our Lyla!"

"Shut up!" she yells back. "Seriously?!"

I run around the car and crouch at her window. "I would never lie about *Silver Falls*. They loved you, Shrupty. The part is yours."

I feel a tap on my shoulder and turn to see Pete, the security guard, frowning at me. "I appreciate the celebration, but people are waiting."

"Sorry, sir!" Shrupty says. She lets her sunglasses fall over her eyes, then says to me, "Get in, loser."

I laugh and run back around to the passenger's side and jump in. She drives out of the exit lane, then turns the corner and pulls to the curb.

"I'm guessing you have to go back in," she says.

"Yeah," I say. "I just wanted to give you the good news in person. Are you excited?"

She chuckles nervously. "I can't believe I actually got it! I honestly thought I had zero chance."

"You were so good," I say. "You blew me—I mean, everyone—away. Really."

She tucks her hair behind her ear. "You're sweet." We lock eyes, and I feel my heart start to race. "What are you doing tonight? I just decided I'm having a celebratory dinner. You should come."

My stomach starts to fizz like a shaken-up soda bottle. Did she just ask me out on a date? No. She said she's having a celebratory dinner, so that means she'll probably invite her friends, too. But still, it's a chance to spend more time with her. I tell myself not to get my hopes up, then immediately start getting my hopes up. Fantasies of us clinking champagne glasses and holding hands along the beach and making out float through my mind. I try to stamp them down by using my worries as water to put out the fire.

The biggest one being: I don't have the money to be going out and celebrating anything.

But as I look at Shrupty, her honeyed eyes melting me as she waits hopefully for my answer, I know I'm screwed. I can't say no to her. I don't want to say no to her.

So, for the first time in my life, I decide to go with my gut and worry about the problems later.

"I'd love to."

CHAPTER TWELVE

After work, I wait outside a restaurant called Golden Ivy in West Hollywood to meet Shrupty and her friends. It's a glamorous-looking place with wide-open windows and vines growing over the blush-pink walls. Santa Monica Boulevard is buzzing with people heading to dinner while music flows out of all the cafés and bars. A group of people around my age walk by me and take one of the outdoor tables, and I wonder if they're Shrupty's friends. My fingers play nervously with the hem of my shirt. I hope her friends like me.

"Bex!" I hear Shrupty call from behind me. I turn to look down the sidewalk, where she emerges from a crowd of people, waving at me.

"Whoa," I mumble to myself when I see her. She looks more gorgeous than ever in high-waisted blue jeans, a yellow lace camisole, and an oversize white bomber jacket. I snap myself out of my daze and wave back.

"I'm so glad you came," she says when she reaches me.

"Of course," I say. "Thank you for inviting me. Is everyone else meeting us out here, or should we go inside?"

She furrows her brow. "Oh, I didn't invite anyone else. It's just us."

"Oh," I say, trying hard to hide my joy at hearing that. I feel my lips threatening to break into a huge grin, so I turn away from her.

That's when I see a familiar face walking toward me. It's Parker, and he's with Dante. Fear hits me in the gut. I don't want Parker to see me here with Shrupty. Being around a girl I like and who might actually like me back is new to me; it's awkward and uncomfortable and makes me more self-conscious than I've ever been in my life. Having Parker hovering over my shoulder during this dinner is only going to amplify all that. Besides, he can read me like a book just by looking at me. What if he figures out I'm into her and I'm forced to come out before I'm ready?

No. I can't let him see me. I have to hide.

"Let's go inside," I say to Shrupty. But just as we're heading to the doors, a group of tall Scandinavian model–types cut in front of us, blocking the entry while they go over the menu hanging in the window.

I glance over my shoulder. Parker and Dante have stopped to pet someone's pug. That buys me a little more time.

"Are you okay?" Shrupty asks.

I give her my best I'm Totally Fine smile. "Yeah. Just, um, hungry."

Parker and Dante are on the move again, walking past the bar next door. Finally, a gap opens in between the models and I go for it.

I sidestep my way through them, using their height as cover. But just as I'm about to make it inside, I slam right into a waiter carrying a tray of drinks. I fall back into the models, knocking them over like bowling pins, and land on the ground with a thud.

"Ugh," I groan as I lie on the concrete, my shirt soaked in chilled rosé and something that smells like lime. Chaos erupts around me. I hear the models consoling one another and helping one another up. My glasses are covered in booze, but I can make out Shrupty's shape as she leans over me.

"Jesus," she gasps. "Are you okay?"

"Bex?" Parker calls from the sidewalk.

Ah, shit. I sit up and take my glasses off to wipe them on my shirt. When I put them back on, I see the models wiping themselves off.

"I'm so sorry," I say to them, feeling so embarrassed I could die.

One or two of them ignore me, but most of the group seem sympathetic. "Don't worry," one of them says. "I'm just glad you're okay! That looked bad."

"Bex!" Parker says again, and now he's standing right next

to me. "I wasn't sure it was you. But then you fell down, and I knew that's definitely my cousin." He laughs but then reaches down to give me a hand.

"Ha, ha," I say sarcastically.

Shrupty helps me up, too, and having her hold my hand even for a brief moment almost makes all this humiliation worth it.

Once I'm on my feet, I see the waiter I ran into sitting in a mess of broken bottles and glasses, the tray on his lap.

He glares at me, and I cringe. "I am so sorry. I didn't see you."

"I was right in front of you," he says as he climbs to his feet.

"I'm so, so sorry," I say again, frowning. I wish I could just melt into the puddles of rosé beneath me and disappear.

Shrupty turns to the waiter. "Hey, Adam, it was an accident, okay?"

His eyebrows shoot up. "Oh, Shrupty. I didn't realize she was with you."

"Well, she is with me." She picks a chunk of lime out of my hair, then turns to another waiter. "Could you please get her a towel so she can clean herself up?"

The waiter scurries to the bar. My eyes dart to Parker, who looks impressed. My cheeks run hot, I'm so embarrassed.

Parker rubs my back gently. "Are you sure you're okay?"

"That looked like it hurt," Dante adds.

I nod but can't look any of them in the eye. "I'm fine. Just completely humiliated. And soaked in alcohol."

Shrupty leans in and sniffs me. "Mm. Smells like lime; I like it." A shiver runs down my spine. Feeling her so close does something to me, makes my heart swell and my skin tingle. But Parker is here, he's watching, and I can't let myself feel this gloriousness right now. This is not how I want him to find out I'm gay.

Parker, seemingly oblivious to my inner turmoil, laughs. "Who is this girl? I like her."

"Oh," I say. "This is Shrupty. My friend." There's a chance I accentuate the word *friend* a little too heavily, because Shrupty looks perplexed. But I forge ahead and gesture to Parker. "Shrupty, this is my cousin, Parker, and this is Dante."

"Nice to meet you," she says, then narrows her eyes at Dante. "I've seen you around."

He smiles, his eyes crinkling in the cutest way. "Yeah. I think we run in the same circles."

Just then, the waiter hurries over with a towel, and I use it to dab at my shirt and hair.

"Do you guys want to join us?" Shrupty asks them. "Bex just helped me land a role on *Silver Falls*, so we're celebrating."

I hold my breath. I'm so tense that the muscles in my neck ache. *Please say no, Parker. Please.*

"I never say no to celebrating," Parker says.

"Great!" Shrupty says. "This is my aunt's restaurant, so we're guaranteed a great table."

Oh, that's why she knows the waiters. So I just made a total fool of myself at her aunt's swanky establishment. Another point to me.

We follow Shrupty through the double doors, past the hostess, who knows Shrupty by name, and through the lounge. Beautiful people drink rosé while chatting on pink velvet fainting couches or seated at the marble bar. Shrupty strolls through the place with an air of confidence about her that makes me swoon. I notice something embroidered on the back of her jacket. It's the word *heartbreaker*. I can't help but smile. The jacket tells no lies.

It's obvious why her Instagram posts are so popular—she has amazing style. Meanwhile, I'm wearing the same outfit I wore to work: black jeans she's seen me in twice already and another one of Parker's button-down patterned shirts—this time it's navy blue with little white bird print on it. But it's not like anyone in here is looking at me anyway, not when Shrupty enters the room.

"Wait here," Shrupty says when we reach the back dining room. "I'll find out what's available."

"This place is fancy as fuck," Dante says quietly.

"I feel like I'm in *Vanderpump Rules*," Parker adds. "Quick, Dante, throw a drink in my face!"

They chuckle while I quietly descend into panic. I'm terrified that Parker will figure out I'm crushing on Shrupty. My body reacts to her in ways I can't control: the blushing, the way I smile when she smiles, the fact that my gaze is always drawn to her. No one else would notice these subtle things, but no one else knows me like Parker. What if he figures out that I like her? What if he asks me if I'm queer?

I want to come out to him, I really do, but I want it to be on my terms. I push my glasses farther up my nose and take in a breath, trying to pull myself together. Maybe I'm over-reacting. Maybe I can just squish my feelings for her all the way down, just for an hour or so.

Shrupty comes around the corner and waves us over. The moment I see her smile, I light up like Times Square on New Year's Eve. How the hell am I going to switch this feeling off?

CHAPTER THIRTEEN

We follow Shrupty outside to what I can only describe as a gothic tea garden. Golden skulls on each table hold pink candles, creating an eerie but intimate vibe. Each table is adorned with black roses in copper teapots. Vines climb up the walls and cover the ceiling, winding around a shimmering chandelier.

"Wow," I say as Shrupty stops at a booth in the back and slides in. "This is your aunt's place? It's so . . ."

"Strange," she says, grinning. "I know. But it's a good strange, right?"

I slide in opposite her, and Parker follows me. Dante sits next to Shrupty.

"I'm really vibing with this goth aesthetic," Parker says, looking around. "It's like being at a romantic funeral."

Shrupty laughs. "Right? I went through a really intense

goth phase in high school. I spent hours back here writing terrible poetry and sneaking absinthe from behind the bar."

"Nice," Dante says as he relaxes into the plush velvet seat.

A waiter comes over to take our drink order. I almost drop the menu when I see how expensive everything is.

Parker nudges me inconspicuously. "Don't look so panicked," he whispers. "I'll put it on my card. Just stick to the cheaper options."

"Thank you," I whisper. "You're the best."

"I know," he says with a smirk and a wink.

I mentally scold myself for getting so caught up in my feelings for Shrupty that I didn't think more about how much this would cost. If Parker weren't here, I'd have to dip into my already limited savings.

I order the cheapest drink on the menu: something called a Roy Rogers. Shrupty gets a virgin Cinderella, Parker orders a hilariously titled Benedict Cucumber Batch, and Dante keeps it simple with a beer.

There's an awkward silence once the waiter leaves. I glance at Shrupty and see her smiling at me, then panic and look at the table instead.

To my relief, Dante starts telling us about his day at a photo shoot in the Valley. Parker interjects every now and then with a joke that makes us all laugh. Even though they've only been hanging out a week or two, I just love them together.

Dante is super chill. He's quiet and reserved, and when he does speak his voice is soft. Just being around him is calming. Parker, on the other hand, is high energy, all the time. Whether he's making snappy one-liners or telling an animated story after a night out, he's always switched on. But even though they're so different, they just fit so well together. It's like they balance each other out. Dante brings P back down to earth, and P brings Dante out of his shell.

By the time the waiter returns with our drinks, I'm feeling much more relaxed about being here with Shrupty.

She looks at me from behind her long lashes as she sips her mocktail. "Thanks so much for coming out with me." She reaches over the table and takes my hand. "I'm so excited to be working with you."

My whole body flushes. "Me too." I tell myself to pull my hand away, but I can't bring myself to do it. I'm torn between protecting my secret and following my heart. So I go with it and hope that Parker is too distracted by Dante's storytelling and dazzling smile to notice.

Her hand lingers on mine a few more seconds, then she slowly pulls it away. I want to reach out and take it back, but I don't. Instead, I decide to make a small but meaningful move by proposing a toast.

"To Shrupty's new role!" I say, holding my glass up. The others lift up their drinks and we all clink them together.

"To Shrupty!" Dante says.

"To new friends," Parker says with a grin.

"So," Dante says to Shrupty. "Is this your first acting role?"

She nods. "I'm kind of terrified. Honestly, I never even expected I'd pass the audition. And that guy was so damn intimidating."

"Malcolm," I say.

"Ah," Parker says, recognizing his name from my midday text rants. "The boss. That's why I love being a freelancer—no assholes telling me what to do all the time."

"What do you do?" Shrupty asks. Her jacket falls down past her shoulder and she lets it hang there. Her brown skin glows in the candlelight, and I have to force myself to look away.

"I'm a makeup and hair stylist," he says. He gestures to Dante. "That's how we met."

"Awww," Shrupty swoons.

"You should have seen him before their first date," I say, nudging Parker playfully. "He was so nervous."

Dante's eyes light up. "He was?"

I nod. "And he couldn't stop smiling when he came home."

"Hush," Parker says, trying to cover my mouth with his hand. I swat it away, giggling. "You're giving away all my secrets."

Dante leans forward over the table, his dreads falling over his face. "I want to know all of your secrets."

Shrupty points at them. "See, that's what I want. You two

have such an obvious connection. It's like you've been together for years."

For the first time in my life, I notice Parker shying away. He bites on his bottom lip and glances away. "Now look what you've done. I'm blushing."

"Aww." I rest my head on his shoulder. "You're so cute."

"You're so lucky to have each other," Shrupty says to us. "My cousins are all older than me, so we're not that close, and my little brother is a nightmare. I wish I was close to him like you two are."

Parker and I look at each other and laugh.

"Trust me," he says. "We've had our moments."

Suddenly, I'm hit with a new terror. We're getting dangerously close to talking about my childhood, and I'm not ready for Shrupty to know about that yet.

"Really?" Shrupty asks.

Parker nods. "We shared a room for most of our lives, and being all up in each other's space like that isn't fun. We fought a lot."

Oh god. I feel frozen, watching helplessly as this conversation veers toward the edge of somewhere I don't want to go.

"Oh," Shrupty says. "You lived together? No wonder you seem more like brother and sister."

"Yep. We're good now," I say, a little too aggressively. "That's what matters."

He nods. "Totally. After our dads both skipped town, our

moms couldn't afford rent, so they moved us all in together. So we're super close."

My panic rises in my chest. I watch Shrupty's reaction, looking for signs of judgment. She grew up surrounded by wealth and Hollywood and glamour. There's no way she'll look at me the same if she finds out I grew up a friendless loner who had to scrape pennies together just to take the bus to work after school every day.

"Should we order some food?" I suggest, trying to change the subject. We all open up our menus, and I breathe a sigh of relief.

"Where did you grow up again?" Shrupty asks. My shoulders tense up.

"Westmill, an hour outside Seattle," Parker says. "Don't feel bad if you've never heard of it. No one has."

Shrupty laughs. Parker starts telling her about how poor we were, and I sink into the cushion of the seat, wishing it would swallow me whole. How do I stop this?

Freaking out, I kick Parker's shin under the table. He winces, then turns to me with a look of shock on his face.

Just then, Shrupty's phone rings. "Sorry, it's my mom. One sec." She answers it, and I take the opportunity to talk to Parker.

"Please don't," I whisper to him.

"Excuse me?" he says. "You 'don't'! You kicked me."

"Because you were telling her how poor we are. I don't want her knowing anything about Westmill. It's embarrassing."

Hurt flashes in his eyes, and his whole body stiffens. "Fine. I'm sorry I'm such an embarrassment to you."

I reach for his hand, but he pulls it away. "No, P. That's not what I meant."

Shrupty ends her call and the table falls silent. The rest of the night is painfully uneventful. Parker hardly says a word. I'm too consumed by guilt to eat, but the food is all so expensive that I force it down so it's not a waste of money. Dante and Shrupty try their best to keep the conversation flowing, but it's clear that the mood has soured, and soon Dante is dropping Parker and me home.

CHAPTER FOURTEEN

"Please don't be mad at me," I say once we're inside.

Parker raises his eyebrows. "You don't get to tell me how to feel right now."

I hold my palms up at him. "Okay, you're right. I'm sorry. And I'm sorry I kicked you."

He avoids looking at me as he walks into the kitchen and opens the fridge. "Honestly, the kick didn't hurt as much as you telling me to shut up."

I crawl onto the futon and wrap myself under the blanket. "You were blabbing about us! I don't want her knowing we got all our clothes from Goodwill or that we lived on food stamps. She wouldn't understand."

He pushes the fridge closed without taking anything out of it, then leans on the counter, glaring at me. "Do you hear how disrespectful you're being right now? Our mothers did everything they could for us. We shouldn't be ashamed of that. Is that why you haven't called your mom once since you arrived?"

I shouldn't be surprised that he knows that. She probably told my aunt, who told him. "That's not—"

He holds a finger up to silence me. "You know what? I'm. Not. Done."

My jaw snaps closed. I don't remember the last time I've seen him this upset.

"Bex, you saw what I went through in high school. You know more than anyone how much hell those bullies put me through. But I always was comforted by the fact that they didn't know me, so they had no right to judge me. They were assholes who projected their own hatred and insecurities onto me. And no matter what they said, I never ever let them make me feel ashamed of who I was. But you . . . You know me better than anyone in the whole world. To see you avert your gaze from me tonight, to hear you say that you were embarrassed by our lives, like you were ashamed of us—*of me* . . ." He takes in a deep breath. "How dare you."

Tears well in my eyes. "I didn't realize—"

He throws his hands in the air. "Whatever. You obviously need to unpack a lot of internalized shit, girl. Because I'm not embarrassed or ashamed about how we grew up, or being from Westmill, or the lives our mothers gave us. And you shouldn't be either."

He walks into his room and closes his door. I sit under my blanket, feeling like the worst person in the world.

I want to stay in bed and give him space, but soon the Roy Rogers I drank is threatening to burst my bladder. I crawl off the futon and tiptoe toward Parker's bedroom door. This is going to be awkward.

I knock quietly, hoping he's already asleep. But then I hear a sad, soft voice reply, "Come in."

When I peek my head in, he's lying in bed with his laptop on his chest, watching something.

"I have to pee," I say sheepishly, my thighs squeezed together like they're holding in a tsunami. "Like, bad."

He nods, and I scurry past him into the bathroom and close the door. When I'm done, I try to sneak out of his room quietly, but just as I'm about to leave he says my name. I spin on my heels and burst into tears.

"I'm . . . so . . . sorryyyy," I cry, covering my face with my hands. Then I kneel down beside his bed and take his hand in mine. "What I said was shitty and selfish and I take it all back. I should never have acted like I'm embarrassed by you, because I'm not. I'm proud to be the one person who knows you better than anyone else."

Parker looks at me with tears in his eyes, then lifts the comforter up. "Get in here."

I wipe my tears and climb in beside him. "I really am so sorry, P."

He nods. "I know you are, and I forgive you. But you better not talk about our mothers like that again, or there'll be trouble."

I hold a hand over my heart. "I swear, it won't happen again."

"Good." He presses the play button on his laptop and an old episode of *Grey's Anatomy* continues. Memories of us watching *I Love Lucy* marathons in bed as children come flooding back, and suddenly I miss my mother so much it makes my heart ache.

"You're right, you know?" I say quietly.

Parker yawns. "About what?"

"I've been ashamed of my life," I say, choking back fresh tears. "It didn't hit me until you said it. And as much as I didn't want to hear it, I know it's true. I've been ashamed of who I am for as long as I can remember."

Just saying those words feels like a release, like opening a door I've kept locked somewhere deep inside me. I cry quietly until the credits roll, letting the pain out one tear at a time. I've been ashamed. But I don't want to hurt myself like that anymore. I don't want to hurt my family like that anymore.

"Parker," I whisper.

He takes in a slow breath. "Hmm?"

I nervously bite down on my bottom lip, tasting the saltiness of my tears. "I have to tell you something." My chest swells with emotion, and I try to stamp it out so I can speak. "I'm gay."

The words leave my lips like a wild bird that has been caged for too long. But Parker doesn't say anything. I wait in silence for what feels like an eternity, panicked thoughts racing through my mind.

"P?" I ask, my voice hoarse from crying. When he still doesn't reply, I realize he's fallen asleep.

He didn't hear me. I finally muster the courage to say those two life-altering words, and no one heard it. I roll over and take my glasses off so I can bury my face in the pillow.

No one heard it. But I said it. And I felt it. Maybe that's all that matters right now.

. . .

I'm making pancakes when Parker walks into the kitchen the next morning, his eyes half-open, creases down the side of his face from sleeping.

"You're up early," he says before yawning loudly.

"I wanted to make you breakfast," I say as I pour more pancake mix into the pan.

"Aww," he says as he drags a barstool out from under the kitchen counter and sits down. I set a place for him at the counter, complete with cutlery, napkins, butter, and maple syrup. I turn so my back is facing him, blocking his sight of the pan. I woke up with a plan, and if he sees it before it's ready, I might chicken out. The creamy mix sizzles as I move the spatula through it, molding it into the letter *G*. The letters *I* and *M* are already stacked on a plate by the stove, and once the *G* has browned just enough, I scoop it up and drop it on top of them.

An *A* and *Y* later, I place the plate on the counter in front of Parker and anxiously hold my breath. He reads it out loud.

"'I'm gay,'" he says, then smiles. "Aww, I am gay! Yay! Gaycakes!"

He pops open the maple syrup and pours it over my coming-out message. I furrow my brow, realizing he thinks it's about him. I wipe my hands on my apron and take in a deep breath.

"Yes," I say. "You are. And so am I."

He tilts his head to the side, his mouth full of the fluffy *G* pancake. "Come again?"

This is getting frustrating. I pinch the bridge of my nose between my thumb and forefinger.

"P," I say with a sigh. "I've literally spelled it out for you."

He looks down at the plate, then back at me, and his eyes narrow. "Are you saying what I think you're saying?"

"Ugh!" I groan. "I'm gay!"

My heart feels like it's lodged in my throat. I said it. I can't possibly make it any clearer.

Parker gently places his knife and fork on the plate. Then he swallows the bite of pancake, picks up the napkin, and dabs his mouth with it. Finally, he looks at me, and it's like I can see this new information turning over in his mind.

The corner of his mouth lifts into a half smile, and he nods. "Yeah, makes sense."

My jaw drops. "Wait. What?"

How am I the more shocked one in this conversation?

Parker pushes the plate to the side and reaches over the counter for my hands. "Bex, I shared a room with you from the ages seven to eighteen; I know you better than anyone. So, yeah, it's not like the thought hasn't crossed my mind once, twice, or three thousand times."

I throw my head back and stare at the ceiling. "Whaaaaat. Why didn't you say anything?"

He pats my hand comfortingly. "Not my place. I knew if you were queer, you'd tell me when you were ready. And yay! That's today!"

He stands up and dances over to me, wrapping his arms around my waist and picking me up. I squeal as he starts spinning, like we're awfully uncoordinated ballroom dancers. But I go with it, spreading my arms out wide.

"This is your Simba moment," he says. Then he starts singing "The Circle of Life" from *The Lion King*, and I can't help myself, I burst into laughter.

. . .

Later, we're in his car driving down the highway to Rosemount Studios, and he starts throwing questions at me.

"Do you have a girlfriend?"

I shake my head. "Nope."

"Ex-girlfriends?"

"Nope. Never even been on a date."

"Wait," he says. "Have you ever kissed anyone?"

"Well," I say, smirking, "I used to kiss my Lexa poster before bed every night."

He laughs. "Lexa from *The 100*?"

"She's a babe." It feels so good to be able to talk about this with him. I've imagined these conversations so many times. "My obsession with Clexa is what got me writing fanfic."

He chuckles. "Reason number 103 I thought you were probably queer, bee-tee-dubs."

We laugh about that until my stomach hurts, and then I sigh.

"But," I say, "to answer your question: No, I've never kissed an actual real-life person before."

"Aww." He pats my leg. "You're so lucky. Think of all the firsts you have ahead of you."

I gaze out the window, letting my imagination take me somewhere else. I picture my first date, my first kiss, my first everything . . . and the only person I want to share those firsts with is Shrupty.

CHAPTER FIFTEEN

I'm in line at the café, waiting to pick up my standing order of coffees for the writers' room, when I notice Malcolm sitting at a table in the corner. Angela, the receptionist in the production building, is sitting across from him. Under the table, she slips off her heels, then drags one of her feet up his leg. I turn away quickly, not wanting to see what happens next. I keep my back to them until my order is ready, then hurry out the door before they see me.

I'm walking down the hall to the writers' room when I notice Andy still in his office, so I knock on the door and pop my head in.

"Are you coming to this morning's meeting?" I ask. "Or do you want your coffee in here?"

He looks up at me from his laptop, his brows pinched together like he's confused. "Oh, you didn't get the e-mail. Malcolm has a breakfast thing, so the meeting was canceled."

"Oh." I stare at the tray of coffees in my hands. I guess I'll just make the rounds to everyone's offices and hand them out. I leave Andy's on his desk, then continue down the hall to Jane. But before I reach her door, I see Malcolm from the window. He's still with Angela, and they're getting into his car. I vaguely remember seeing something online about him being married. Maybe Angela is his wife, and I just never put two and two together.

I knock on Jane's door and she calls me in. "Coffee?" I ask, and she slumps back in her chair.

"Oh thank god," she groans. "You're an angel." I hand a cup to her, and she breathes it in.

"I just heard the meeting was canceled," I say.

She nods. "Malcolm has some big important breakfast with an exec or something." She puts the coffee down, then starts sorting through a pile of papers on her desk like she's looking for something. "You'd think he would've given me a heads-up. I could've easily led the room without him for one day. But nope, no one is allowed to even talk about story ideas unless he's there."

"Wait," I say. "An exec? I just saw him leaving with Angela." The second the words leave my mouth, I regret them. I don't want to start any drama—especially drama that involves Malcolm.

Jane's jaw drops. "Angela? Front desk Angela?"

"Yeah. I didn't realize they were married."

Jane drops her face in her hands and groans.

"What?" I ask, feeling very confused but also somehow certain that I've said something I shouldn't have.

Jane looks up at me, and I'm surprised to see she's laughing. Cackling, even.

"Bex, honey," she says, shaking her head at me. "You are too pure for this town. Malcolm is married. But Angela is not his wife."

"Oh," I say, frowning. "*Oh.*"

"Yup." She pushes her hands through her hair, looking frazzled. "Jesus, shit. I bet this is why he's been slacking more than usual lately. I thought he was just burned-out. God dammit."

With another, longer groan, Jane stands up from her desk and picks up her handbag and the coffee. I step aside as she passes, not wanting to get in her way. "I swear to god, if it wasn't for me, this show would never make it to air on time. And Ruby just left for New York for a week of back-to-back meetings, so Malcolm is going to check out like he always does when she's away. I am a ball of stress." She speeds down the hall like a tornado, then stops halfway and turns around. "Are you coming? We've got work to do."

I jump to attention and hurry to catch up to her, listening quietly as she talks about how crappy Malcolm is. I'm not gonna lie, I enjoy every juicy insult.

"If I was showrunner," she says, "we'd be in the room together all day. Breaking story ideas, working on outlines, writing scenes. It would be a democracy, not a dictatorship."

We arrive on set, where I take script notes and get drinks and run errands. I'm on my way to Archer's trailer to tell him he's needed on set, when I see Shrupty walking across the lot, looking a little confused. I take a quick detour to go talk to her, and she smiles when she sees me.

"Oh thank god!" she says. "I'm so lost."

"What are you doing here?" I ask.

"I just did a wardrobe fitting for Lyla," she says, twisting her long hair in her fingers. "And Alyssa asked me to stop by her trailer. She's got some time between filming and wants to start rehearsing our scenes for next week." She lifts her arms in the air, gesturing to the chaos around us. "But this place is a maze."

"I'm headed to the trailers right now," I say, pointing behind me. "I can show you the way."

"Oh, thanks! You're super familiar with this script, right?"

"Yeah, I'm familiar with it," I say. An understatement. Malcolm never did get my name added to the script cover, and Dirk won't reply to my e-mails about it, so I can't really take any credit for it publicly yet.

She takes her sunglasses off and bites her bottom lip like she's unsure of something. "Would I be asking too much if I asked you to help me go over my lines? I'm staying late tonight to keep rehearsing with Alyssa in between shooting, and I'd feel so much better about my performance if you were there to guide me."

"I'd love to!" I say, perhaps a touch too enthusiastically. "I mean, sure. I can swing by. I don't know how much help I'll be, though."

She breathes a sigh of relief. "Thank you so much."

I take her to Alyssa's door just as she's stepping out with Will.

"Um," I say, shuffling my feet from side to side awkwardly. "I gotta go, but I'll meet you back here later?"

Shrupty smiles, and my heart wants to reach out and hug her. "Can't wait."

I turn and walk away, smiling to myself. She said she can't wait. Like she can't wait to see me? Or she can't wait to rehearse? Damn these cryptic lesbian linguistics. How does anyone get together in this world? It's way more confusing than they make it look in rom-coms.

I reach Archer's trailer, but it takes a few knocks before I hear movement inside. He's mid-yawn when he opens it, and his hair is flat on one side, like he's been napping.

"What's up?" he asks as he stretches his arms in the air.

"You're due on set," I say. He steps out and swings his door closed behind him.

"Can I get a green juice?" he asks. "I need fuel." I'm about to answer when he notices Will chatting with Alyssa and Shrupty.

"Oh," he says with a smirk. "The new girl's here. I've seen some of her videos on YouTube. Do you know if she's single?"

My skin prickles. "Shrupty? You know she's, like, über gay, right?" I'm surprised he doesn't know that; Shrupty is super open about it online.

He does a double take. "Jeez, look at that." He nods toward the three of them, watching like he's found a rare Pokémon. "They're all gay. I guess this is what it feels like to be a minority." He laughs, then nudges me with his elbow when I don't laugh. "Us straights better stick together."

I break into a sweat. I desperately want to correct him. I want to pat him on the back, say something witty like "You're on your own, bud," then walk over to join the others. I want to call him out for thinking he has any idea what it's like to be a minority . . . but I can't.

The fact that he felt the need to point out that three queer people are having a conversation, like it's a novelty or something to be gawked at, doesn't make me feel like I can trust him with my own queerness. I don't know if I'm ready to declare it proudly to someone who might not be receptive to it. So I grit my teeth as he erases my sexuality and cracks jokes about it. And then I go fetch a green juice for him, the whole time kicking myself for not speaking up.

CHAPTER SIXTEEN

INT. SASHA'S APARTMENT—NIGHT

Sasha enters. She walks into her kitchen, opens the fridge, and takes out a beer. A shadow moves in the background that she doesn't see. She closes the fridge, pops the cap off the bottle, and takes a sip as she walks into the living room. Another shadow moves behind her that she doesn't see. She puts the beer down, then turns suddenly and pins the intruder against the wall, her knife to their throat.

                  LYLA

You're good.

                    SASHA

Better than you, hunter.

                    LYLA

I'm not here to kill you. Don't get
your tail in a twist.

                    SASHA

Then what do you want from me?

                    LYLA

I'll tell you. But first you need
to get your blade off of my neck.

Sasha hesitates.

                    LYLA

Come on. Why would I let you go if
I wanted you dead?

Sasha slowly pulls the knife away, then
backs off.

                    SASHA

You'll forgive me if I don't trust
so easily. That's a side effect of

```
people constantly trying to kill
you.


Lyla smirks, rubs her neck where the
knife was.


                LYLA
    Trust me, if I wanted to kill you,
    you'd be dead.
```

"Wait," Shrupty says, breaking character. "Should I sound smug when I say that? Or more determined?"

I look up from the script in my lap. I'm in Alyssa's trailer, cross-legged on the couch while they stand in the middle of the room, going over their lines.

"Smug determination?" Alyssa suggests, then chuckles. "Is that a thing?"

"Definitely. Think about why she's there," I say. "She suspects that the people who raised her and loved her growing up are actually the people who killed her parents. She's questioning everything she's ever known and seeking the help of someone she was always told was the enemy. Lyla is conflicted but knows she needs to find out the truth."

Alyssa leans against the kitchen counter, watching me. "You really know this character. Did Malcolm tell you all that?"

Oh shit. That's right; no one else knows that I wrote this episode, that Lyla is my character. I want to tell them, but I'm afraid they won't believe me. Who would believe an intern over the showrunner? "It was discussed when the writers were tabling the script."

I take my phone out and send Dirk yet another e-mail asking him to credit me on 612, making sure to CC Malcolm.

Alyssa holds the script close to her chest. "I'm so in love with this episode. I can't wait till the fans see it." She grins at the thought. "Their minds are going to explode, for real."

Seeing her so excited about it gives me butterflies. "I hope so."

"I never thought Sasha would be canonically gay," she continues. "I've been begging Malcolm to finally confirm her queerness for months, but I never expected he would literally write her a romance. I guess he deserves more credit than I gave him."

I wince a little. I want to tell her that he deserves exactly *none* of the credit. But seeing how happy it's already making Alyssa fills me with pride. If it means that much to her, I can't imagine how fans are going to react. I should focus on what's important: that this episode gets made.

Shrupty sits down next to me, her forehead crinkled with worry. She's so tense that her shoulders are hunched, like she's trying to curl up into a ball. I relate to her so much right now.

Someone knocks on the door, and Alyssa goes to answer it and steps outside.

"Hey," I say quietly to Shrupty. "Just FYI, you're doing amazing. You know, in case you're filled with horrifying self-doubt right now."

She laughs, and I feel a sense of triumph knowing that I made her smile. I want to do it again.

"Is it that obvious?" she asks, scrunching her nose up.

I shake my head. "To the average person, no. But I have a sixth sense for this. I can spot anxiety from a mile away." I raise an eyebrow smugly. "It's a side effect of living with debilitating anxiety myself. I can sense my own kind."

"Heh," she says. "That's a weird superpower to have. Mine is falling in love with totally unavailable people."

I rest my elbows on my knees. "I guess that means I have two weird superpowers then, because same."

Shrupty lifts her hand to her chest and starts playing with her necklace. The pendant looks to be an emerald, surrounded by tiny silver spheres in a floral design. It hangs on the end of a delicate silver chain, long enough for the emerald to sit just above her cleavage.

"That's really beautiful," I say, gesturing to the necklace.

She holds it out gently and gazes down at it. "Thanks. It's a family heirloom from India. My grandmother gave it to me before she died." The emerald shines in the light as she turns it. "It was a brooch originally, but I wanted to wear it all the time, so my mom had it made into a necklace. I never ever take it off."

I can tell her family means a lot to her, and a pang of guilt hits my stomach for being so dismissive of my own lately. I've been waiting for a good time to call Mom so we can have a real conversation, but something always gets in the way. Or maybe I'm still working up the courage to actually hit that call button.

"Do you have any heirlooms?" she asks me, genuinely interested. "Anything that gets passed down from generation to generation?"

I try not to laugh. Yeah, sure, like overwhelming debt, mental illness, and skin that freckles and burns when it's touched by sunlight.

"Nope," I say.

She gives me a curious look. "You don't like to reveal too much about yourself, do you?"

I open the script again and clear my throat. "Not that much to reveal."

Just then, Alyssa returns, holding a bouquet of flowers and a dessert box. She's smiling so wide I can see her wisdom teeth. I'm grateful for the interruption.

"Oooh!" Shrupty coos. "Someone's popular!"

Alyssa giggles. "They're from Charlie. It's our two-year anniversary today." Like Alyssa, her girlfriend, Charlie Liang, made it big on YouTube before moving into acting.

Shrupty and I both swoon.

"You girls are seriously couple goals for me," I say.

Alyssa puts the flowers on the dining table and sits on the chair across from us. "You're queer, right, Bex?"

I jolt back slightly, surprised by her question. No one has ever straight-up asked me that before. I'm not mad, though, because I've been trying to figure out a way to work this into a conversation with Shrupty for days.

"Yeah," I say. "How'd you know?"

"My gaydar never fails," she says with a smirk.

Shrupty stares down at the pages in her lap. "I guess mine has malfunctioned, because I wasn't so sure." I turn to her, wondering what that means. Has she been trying to figure out if I'm queer? She grimaces, like she said something she shouldn't have, then scrambles to explain. "I mean, um, not that I was trying to find out. Or that it matters. Should we take this scene from the top?"

I feel a smile tugging at my lips, but I manage to suppress it. I don't know if I'm reading too much into it, but I think I've been on her mind more than I realized. Maybe I have a chance with Shrupty, after all.

Just then, my phone buzzes with a text from my mom.

Mom: how are you, honey?

I'm about to slide my phone back into my pocket, but then I think of everything Parker said when we fought, and Shrupty talking about her grandmother, and I have to reply.

Bex: good! Working. I'll call you later.

Mom: oh yay! Yes I'd love to hear your voice.
Xo

That just makes my guilt even worse. I never meant to ignore her for so long; it's just with everything that's been happening, Westmill couldn't be further from my mind. Or maybe . . . maybe I want it to be out of my mind. Maybe Parker was right about me, maybe I am ashamed. And instead of dealing with it, I've been trying to forget about it.

But it's not just that. There's also the fact that I still haven't come out to her. And now that I'm here in LA, trying to live an openly gay life, I'm worried about how hard it's going to be to pretend to be straight when I speak to her. I'm scared it will feel like I'm taking a step backward, like I'm retreating into the shell that I've been using all my courage to shatter. I don't know if I'm ready for Mom to ask me if I've met any nice boys here. I don't want to lie to her, but I'm not ready to be honest, either. So right now, it's easier to disappear. Just for a little while.

"I'm due on set soon," Alyssa says as she checks the time on her phone. "I think it's going to be a long night. Hope y'all don't mind waiting on set; we can keep rehearsing during my breaks."

Shrupty nods. "Totally cool with me. I'm excited to come to set with you and watch the magic happen." She looks at me, waiting for my answer. Once again, I find myself unable to say no to her.

"Bring on the long night."

CHAPTER SEVENTEEN

Later, I'm sitting in a golf cart outside the set, replying to comments on the *Silver Falls* Instagram account and eating my homemade PB&J, when Shrupty slides in next to me, in the driver's seat.

"Hey!" she says. "Lunch break?" I nod, still chewing on my last bite. "I've always wanted to drive one of these." She looks around, then gives me a mischievous grin and clutches the steering wheel. "Let's take it for a spin!"

I almost choke on my sandwich. Before I can protest, she's turned the key in the ignition and we're rolling down the street.

"What if someone needs this?" I ask, meaning the golf cart. Shrupty shrugs. "There were two others nearby. Besides, we won't be long. I just want to explore this place a little so I don't get lost again."

I don't argue because I've been wanting to sneak away and explore the studios since my first day. And yeah, okay, I'll take any excuse to spend some one-on-one time with Shrupty. She follows the road until the crowds of crew and visitors ease and we reach the studio back lots.

"This is where they film *Cooper Street*," I say as we drive into Kinney Village. It's like a little suburb, with picturesque Craftsman-style houses that many beloved characters have called home over the years. These days, it's home to bored housewives who find themselves embroiled in one neighborhood scandal after another. My mom is obsessed with that show, so I ask Shrupty to stop so I can snap some quick photos for her.

Then we follow the road out of the 'burbs, around Rosemount Square, with its clock tower, which has been the backdrop for dozens of blockbuster films, and into New York Street.

Shrupty hits the brakes. "Wow! This looks eerily like my street on the Upper East Side."

"You have a place in New York?" I ask, impressed.

"My parents do," she says. "But we don't spend as much time there as we used to. Not since we bought our Paris place."

A place in Beverly Hills, Manhattan, and Paris? Whoa. Three homes? My family didn't even have three bedrooms. Our entire bungalow could probably fit in her closet. My heart sinks as I realize just how out of my league this girl is. I don't stand a chance.

She keeps driving until we come across Davenport Lake, which is actually just a pond with an über-realistic painted backdrop. In real life, it doesn't look that great, but if you film it from very specific angles it creates the illusion of a gorgeous, expansive lake, surrounded by pine trees.

"Do you mind if we chill here for a sec?" she asks.

"Sure," I say. "But I should probably get back to Jane soon."

She nods and steps out of the golf cart. I follow as she walks to the edge of the lake and sits down on the grass. Her hair flows in the breeze, and I find myself staring at her instead of the famous scenery around us.

"Is this what it looks like where you're from?" she asks when I sit next to her. I freeze.

"Um." I look at the wall of fake trees, thinking about how the nicest park in Westmill was practically just a patch of dead grass and a rusted swing set you needed a tetanus shot to use. "Not really." I desperately need to change the subject so she doesn't ask me any questions about my life, so I quickly add, "Are you feeling better after watching some of the filming?"

"Ugh." She pulls her knees up to her chest. "I dunno. I hope I'll be good enough. But, like, I've never done anything like this before, so I'm worried I'm just going to look like a giant, talentless loser."

"I can definitely relate to that," I say. It's comforting to know that even with all her money and fame, she still deals with self-doubt just like me. "But you killed the auditions, and you have great chemistry with Alyssa, so I fully believe you're gonna blow everyone away as Lyla."

She smiles and pushes her hair behind her ear—something I've noticed she does whenever I give her a compliment. "I hope so. Having you there to offer feedback helped a lot."

I cringe a little. "I doubt that. I'm no actor."

"No," she says. "You're a writer. And that's why I asked you for help. You know the script front to back. You know the show. You know what Malcolm and the writers have planned for Lyla and Sasha. I need that genius."

My cheeks flush. She called me a writer *and* a genius in one breath. Wow.

She leans back on her elbows and stares up at the sky. "I guess I'm just nervous. I feel a lot of responsibility to get this character right, you know? It's not every day that a gay Indian girl gets to play a gay Indian girl. And the fact that Lyla is going to have a romance arc with Sasha, a queer black girl played by a queer black girl . . . and neither of them die at the end? That's huge. I want to make sure I do it justice."

I nod along, agreeing with every word she says. "I wish it wasn't so rare."

Shrupty scoffs. "Believe me, so do I. But we'll get there." She raises her fist and I bump it with mine. "We'll get there."

When we both rest our hands back on the grass, our pinkie fingers touch. My first instinct is to jerk my hand away, but then I think . . . What if I don't? What if I just let it be? So I keep my hand still, relishing the feel of her skin against mine, even if it's barely an inch of contact. Shrupty doesn't move her hand, either. My heart flutters. Does this mean something?

I glance down at our pinkies. Mine is chubbier than hers, with nails I've stress-chewed into nothing. Her nails are perfectly manicured and painted a turquoise that pops against her brown skin. I'm still staring at our fingers when she moves hers closer to mine. I'm so surprised that I almost jump. I look up at her, expecting her to be watching the water, but she's looking right back at me from behind her long, dark lashes. She gives me a slow smile. My heart beats like a drum.

If this were a TV show, I'd be so smooth right now. I'd lean in just slow enough to build suspense. Shrupty would lean in, too, closing her eyes in anticipation. Our mouths would meet softly, then the passion between us would grow more intense, and so would the kiss. Sun flares would cast a gorgeous natural light on us, making our silhouettes glow. A cool breeze would gently sway our hair, but not enough to get in the way of our lips melting together. Our kiss would be romantic, sweet, gentle but powerful. It would be perfect. An epic queer soundtrack would play over us, maybe a Janelle Monáe song. Ahh. It would be so dreamy.

But this isn't a TV show. Nancy Meyers is not writing or directing my life. This is the back lot of Rosemount Studios. The sun is hidden behind smog, the air is sticky and hot, and I am incapable of being chill or smooth in any situation. I'm sweaty and anxious and too worried about my peanut butter breath to even utter a word. And besides, what if she doesn't want to kiss me? Consent is an important thing. I'd want to ask her before I ever did anything like that. And I'm not asking until I'm absolutely positive that she likes me back. The only problem with that strategy is that she would have to literally say, to my face, without a hint of sarcasm or joking grin, "Bex, I like you." And even then, I don't think I'd actually believe it.

So I break our lingering stare. I pull my hand away. And I stand up from our little patch of grass by the fake lake.

"We should get going," I say. "My lunch break is over, and someone probably needs me on set. Those green juices aren't going to fetch themselves." I chuckle, but Shrupty hardly cracks a smile.

"Sure," she says quietly. Then we walk back to the golf cart, climb in, and drive to the soundstage in silence.

CHAPTER EIGHTEEN

It's 6:00 a.m. when the director finally calls "cut" and the episode is wrapped. I've spent most of the night balancing intern duties with helping Shrupty rehearse. We haven't spoken about anything that isn't work-related since the lake, and I'm a bundle of confusion and regret and heartache. I keep replaying the moment in my mind like I'm watching a scene in the editing bay. Pausing it at moments that seem so clearly obvious to me now, but at the time I didn't notice. Zooming in on the tiny movements she made that could have been signals. The fingers touching. The lingering looks. The sweet smile.

And then there was me, sitting there beside the most amazing girl I've ever met, and instead of making a move I obsessed over all the reasons it wasn't a perfect moment. What the hell was I waiting for? A director to shout "action"?

The sun is rising before I finally admit to myself that I

fucked up. I should have kissed her. But I didn't, and I have a sinking feeling that I lost her forever. She's hardly been able to make eye contact with me all night.

"I need a nap," she says as we walk back to Alyssa's trailer.

"You can crash on my couch until the table read," Alyssa says. "I've got a breakfast date with Charlie, so you'll have it all to yourself."

Shrupty lets out a drawn-out yawn. "Thanks."

I don't care how sleep-deprived I am, there's no way I'm missing the table read for the episode I wrote. Even if no one else knows I wrote it but me and Malcolm.

Alyssa says a quick good-bye, then heads toward the parking lot. I keep walking with Shrupty, racking my tired brain for something to say.

"Did you have a good night?" I ask, then feel kind of silly about it.

She yawns again. "Yeah. It was intense, but I loved seeing how it all works behind the scenes. I can't wait to start filming next week." We stop in front of Alyssa's trailer, and she reaches for my hand, then stops herself and pulls away. "Thanks again for staying back to help me."

Okay. She almost just held my hand. I saw that. I'm not imagining it or reading too much into it. Not this time. Now's my chance to let her know I like her back. I hold my breath, then reach out and take her hand in mine. "My pleasure."

Shrupty glances down at our linked fingers, then looks up

at me. A surprised smile grows on her face. "Um. I guess I'll see you at the table read?"

I nod, then she opens the door to the trailer. But we don't let go.

"Bye," I say, smiling. "Sleep well."

"Thanks," she says. She takes the first step up, then the next, and we still don't let go. Even when she yawns for the third time.

"You're tired," I say. "I'll let you get some rest."

She stifles yet another yawn. "Okay. You're right."

We both look down at our hands that won't let go of each other, and giggle.

"Okay," she says. "Good night." I can tell she's not going to let go by the twinkle in her eye, but my anxiety is starting to rise. I'm not used to these feelings. And I'm especially not used to having these feelings reciprocated. So I slowly, gently slide my fingers away from hers.

"'Night," I say. I wait until she closes the door, then spin on my heels and fist pump the air. "Yessss!"

To my horror, I hear Shrupty giggling from the window. She just saw me celebrate holding her hand.

"You saw nothing!" I call to her.

"I saw everything!" she calls back, laughing harder.

"Gotta go! Byeeeeee!" I walk away as fast as I can, embarrassed but also totally giddy.

. . .

I arrive to the table read ten minutes early to set up the snacks, bags of pastries hanging off my arms. I already ate one on the way; I was starving and I like to take my meds with food so they digest easier. Malcolm is seated at the head of the table, highlighting lines in our script.

"I come bringing gifts," I say to the gathering cast members as I lay the Danishes, macarons, and doughnuts on the middle of the long table. I've barely emptied the bags before half of them are gone. I'm snapping a photo of the table to post to the *Silver Falls* Instagram later, when Malcolm spits out some of the lemon Danish he just bit into.

"This is stale. Who did this?!" He looks around at everyone in the room, easily upward of twenty people, like he's King Joffrey demanding the head of a Stark.

"Well?" he roars. "Who brought these stale, disgusting pastries into my table read?"

I gulp my fear down and slowly raise my hand.

His eyes widen. "Of course it was you. Where did you get these from?"

"They're from the café," I say, my voice quiet. "Here on the lot."

"Your incompetence just hit a new level," he says as he wipes crumbs off his hands. "If you knew anything, you would know that we use Bluebird Bakery in Burbank for our pastries. Why are you even here? You can't even get a simple task like picking up baked goods right. You're useless. Get out. And take these bullshit excuses for food with you." He throws his half-eaten Danish at me, hitting me in the chest. Trembling, I scoop the rest of the pastries into the bags and run out of there as fast as I can.

On my way out the door, I bump into Shrupty. I can't even look at her, I'm so shaken up.

"What the hell was that about?" she asks. My voice fails me, so I try to give her a look that says "don't ask" as I shuffle past. She takes me by the elbow, gently, so I can't run away. "Bex? Was someone just screaming at you?"

"It's fine," I say. "Part of the job. Sorry, I gotta go."

She tries to talk to me some more, but I'm afraid that if I stay any longer, I'll cry. I dump the pastries in the trash and escape to the nearest bathroom, where I stay until I can breathe again.

When I finally emerge, the table read is over and everyone is getting back to work. I creep onto the set like a skittish mouse, strategically walking alongside clothing racks as people from wardrobe push them around. When I get inside the sound-stage, I stand behind set walls and props and monitors until I'm sure the coast is clear. Malcolm is nowhere to be found. Thank god.

Alyssa is talking to the director about the scene they're getting ready to film. Jane is a cowriter with Andy on this week's episode, so they're both sitting in their chairs, ready to roll. I stretch my neck and shake out my shoulders, trying to physically release the anxiety that is crushing me like a boa constrictor. Then I walk over to Jane, putting on my best Everything Is Fine smile.

"There you are," she says. She smiles like she's happy to see me, and my shoulders relax a little. "I was worried when you weren't at the table read. Are you okay?"

"Yeah," I lie.

Andy leans forward to talk to me. "I hear Mal ripped into you pretty bad."

My stomach twists itself into a knot, but I try to laugh it off. "I'm fine."

Jane touches my arm. "I'm sorry. He's in a mood today for some reason. Just ignore him."

Why is it that when assholes act like assholes, everyone else just has to ignore it? It doesn't make him less of an asshole. It just gives him the power to take it up a notch.

Jane pulls an envelope out of her folder and hands it to me. "Could you please run this over to the mail room?"

"Sure," I say, then take the envelope and leave the soundstage.

"Bex!" a voice calls from behind me as I walk through the lot. I know it's Shrupty before I even turn around. "I've been looking everywhere for you."

She speed-walks over to me, carrying a coffee from the café. "Did you get my texts?"

I vaguely remember my phone buzzing in my pocket while I was melting down in the bathroom. I didn't want to check my phone in case it was my mom scolding me for not calling her like I said I would. "I must have missed them. Sorry."

"As long as you're okay," she says. Then she holds the coffee out to me. "Here. I, um, brought you a coffee. As a thank-you for staying up all night helping me rehearse."

I'm so grateful, I could cry. "Thank you so much. You have no idea how much I need this." We linger for a moment, smiling at each other. "Um. Do you want to walk with me?" I hold the letter up. "I need to take this to the mail room. Intern duties."

She beams at me. "I'd love to." I've never seen anyone more excited to deliver mail. It's kind of sweet.

"So," I say, trying to come up with conversation. "How was the table read?"

Shrupty shrugs. "I think it went okay? I've never done one before, so I have nothing to compare it to. But that Malcolm guy was pissed about something, so everyone was super tense."

I shake my head. "He's such a tyrant."

"But," she continues, "Will lightened the mood with some jokes. And then he invited everyone to his birthday party this Saturday."

Dammit. I missed out on an invite to a star-studded celebrity bash.

"He said his boyfriend is throwing him a huge party," she explains. "Will doesn't know anything about it except that it's on Saturday at eight P.M., at some warehouse in the Valley."

"Aww, man," I moan. "That sounds so cool."

"Right?" Shrupty takes her hair out of the topknot it was in, letting it fall down over her shoulders. "Are you gonna go?"

I frown. "I mean, I didn't get an invite, so . . ."

She nudges me playfully with her shoulder. "You could come with me?"

"Oh." I try not to smile, but I can't help it. "Really?"

Shrupty looks away shyly. "You could be my date. If you want?"

I inhale sharply. My heart pauses, like it's listening, waiting to hear what my answer will be. "I'd love that."

CHAPTER NINETEEN

"How cute are we?" Parker asks as he buckles his belt of makeup brushes around his hips. "I feel like we're in a nineties rom-com."

I laugh so hard I almost slip off the stool I'm sitting on. We're in front of the bathroom mirror, about to do my makeup and hair for my date with Shrupty. Parker has always loved doing my makeup, and I was the perfect guinea pig for him to practice on growing up. So when he offered to be my one-man glam squad tonight, of course I said yes.

"Are you freaking out about your date?" Parker asks, grinning.

My cheeks flush and I look down at my shoes. "Maybe a little. I've never been on a date before. I've never even had anyone I liked like me back before." I chuckle uncomfortably, and he pouts.

"First dates are so awkward," he says sympathetically. "But try to enjoy it. That way, if nothing comes of it with Shrupty, at least you'll have had fun."

I nod, taking his advice to heart. "I think we'll have fun. We've had fun every other time we've hung out."

"See?" he says, smiling. "You have nothing to worry about. She obviously likes you." He pauses to choose an eye shadow palette. "Smoky eye, cat eye, *au naturale*? Preferences?"

I shrug my hands up. "Smoky, I guess? And what do you mean she obviously likes me?"

He puts his hands on his hips. "She couldn't take her eyes off you at the Golden Ivy the other night." He clips my hair back, and I notice him giggling to himself.

"What?" I ask.

He starts laughing. "I knew she was queer straightaway."

My whole body tingles thinking about Shrupty watching me at the Golden Ivy. But something P said pushes me to ask something I've been wondering since I came out to him.

"When did you first think I might be gay?"

He thinks for a moment, then chuckles. "Midnight screening of *Eclipse*." I give him a quizzical look, and he explains. "Don't you remember? I asked if you were Team Edward or Team Jacob, and you said—"

"Team Bella," I say, remembering. We both laugh. "Kristen Stewart was absolutely the catalyst for my sexual awakening."

Parker sighs happily. "Mine was Edward Cullen. I wanted to be his spider monkey."

It feels so good to be talking about this with someone who gets it . . . Hell, it feels good just to be talking about it at all. How did I hold all this in before? And what the hell was I so worried about?

"Close your eyes," he says as he dips his eye shadow brush into light brown shadow. I do as he asks, then feel the soft hairs of the brush sweep over my lids.

"Have you always known you're gay?" he asks.

"No," I say. "I think that's one of the reasons I didn't label myself for so long. At first I thought maybe I'm bi, but gay feels more accurate now. You always knew, right?"

He nods. "But everyone always knew with me. I came out of the womb with a pride flag wrapped around my little pink butt."

I laugh so hard that I almost fall off the stool again.

"Still," I say once I can breathe. "It wasn't easy for you. I remember all the homophobia you had to deal with in town."

His smile fades. "That's why I wanted to do this. I wish I had someone to make me feel pretty and tell me it's all gonna be okay."

I look at him in the mirror. "Thanks, P."

"It is, you know," he says softly.

"Hmm?"

"It's gonna be okay."

. . .

"Are you sure this is the right place?" I ask as we creep down the alleyway. The only light is from a flickering lamppost back on the street and the fading headlights of the car that dropped us off. Shrupty takes teeny-tiny steps along the cracked, uneven path.

"Valentino heels were not meant for this cruelty," she says.

We walk a few more feet, and just as I'm about to check the address again, I hear voices on the other side of the fence. I peer through a gap in the fence and see two big, buff guys in tight black shirts standing by the door of a warehouse.

"This way, ladies," one of them says.

Shrupty and I glance at each other. "Um, is this Will's party?" she calls to them.

One of them opens the door, and a flood of music hits us.

"You're at the right place," the other says. "Don't be shy."

I let Shrupty step through first, then we follow the thumping bass into the building. I knew Will's boyfriend, Ryan, had kept this party under wraps to keep the paparazzi out, but I never expected it would be like this. I felt cool just for getting an invite, but sneaking down a dingy alleyway and into a secret warehouse party takes it to another level. For the first time in my life, I'm one of the cool kids. I could get used to this.

We walk down a long graffiti-covered hallway toward a set

of double doors and yet another big guy in a tight shirt. He sees us coming and opens the doors.

"Have a great night, girls," he says as we enter.

"Whoa," I say once we're finally inside.

Shrupty giggles. "I don't think we're in the Valley anymore, Toto."

It doesn't even feel like we're in a warehouse anymore. It's like a winter wonderland. An ice-skating rink is in the center of the building, already busy with guests. Disco balls and colorful spotlights hang over the rink, bathing us in pinks and blues and yellows. To the right of us is a counter to hand over our coats and bags and pick up some skates. To the left is a cocktail bar built out of large blocks of ice—literal ice. A digital screen behind the bar boasts a temperature of minus ten degrees. A dance floor has been set up behind it, and I see some familiar faces there.

"I should have dressed warmer," Shrupty says, looking down at her black off-the-shoulder minidress and denim jacket.

I point to the guests sitting in the ice-sculpted booths, wearing white coats. "They have jackets at the bar."

She makes a face. "I look too good to cover this up." She runs a hand down the side of her torso. My mouth goes dry.

"Facts," I say without thinking, then immediately start to blush. But it's true; she's stunning. Tonight, her hair is swept to one side, showing off a silver-and-emerald ear cuff on her right lobe that matches her grandmother's antique necklace, which she's also wearing. Dark eyeliner sweeps along her lashes, forming a cat-eye wing at the end. Warm gold eyeshadow shines on her upper and lower lids, highlighting the subtle hints of green in her eyes. And her lips, wow, her lips are a dark brown, almost purple color.

Standing next to her in my—you guessed it—black skinny jeans and an old striped men's shirt I found at Goodwill last year, I feel underdressed. But at least my makeup and hair are on point. P introduced me to the wonderful world of contouring, so I'm pretty sure my highlighter is popping under these lights.

"Thanks," Shrupty says. "You look very handsome, too."

Handsome. Whoa. No one has ever called me handsome before. I like the way it feels, so much that I wish I could put it on a button and wear it proudly.

"Thank you," I say with a happy sigh.

She smiles at me, then loops her arm in mine and walks us over to Will and Ryan, who are living it up on the dance floor.

"Happy birthday!" I say when we reach him.

He gives me a bear hug. "Thank you! I'm so happy you came!"

He introduces me to Ryan, even though he needs no introduction. He's the guitarist in the most popular band in the country right now, the Brightsiders. Their queer anthems make up most of my playlist.

Just then, Chloe and Emmy jump onto the dance floor to

say hi. It was Chloe's party where Shrupty and I first met, and Emmy is the drummer from the Brightsiders and bandmate of Ryan. Everyone seems to know everyone else in this town.

"This is Bex," Shrupty yells over the music to them.

Chloe raises their eyebrows. "Ohhh, *this* is Bex! I've heard about you."

"Really?" I ask them, surprised.

"Oh, yeah," they say, exchanging a smirk with Emmy. "Shrupty can't go five minutes without mentioning your name."

Hearing that makes me want to squeal with joy. That has to mean Shrupty likes me . . . right? Talking about someone nonstop is definitely a sign that you have a thing for them. But I can't hush that voice in my head telling me not to get my hopes up. Maybe Shrupty has been talking about me because she's excited about working on *Silver Falls*.

Shrupty grabs Chloe's hand and squeezes it. "You're freaking her out!"

Chloe puts an arm around her. "My apologies." But then they wink at me and grin.

"Okay," Shrupty says, taking my hand. "We're going skating."

"We are?" I ask, but she doesn't hear me over the music.

We're strapped into our skates and about to step onto the ice before I finally work up the courage to tell her I've never skated a day in my life. The closest I've ever been to any kind of skating is when Gabby's cousin gave us tickets to see her compete in Roller Derby.

"Stick with me," Shrupty says with a sexy wink. "I've got you."

A shiver runs down my spine, and I don't know if it's from the cold temperatures or from her winking at me like that. But I'm ready to follow her anywhere.

I take slow, careful steps onto the ice. With my knees slightly bent and my hands out in front of me, I must look like a toddler taking their first awkward steps. Alyssa and her girlfriend, Charlie, glide over like two queer angels.

"How amazing is this?" Charlie asks. "A freaking ice-skating rink!"

They start talking about how cool it is, but all I can think about is how much money this must have cost. Probably more than my mom's earned in her whole life. I can't lie, it annoys me. I'm bitter about it. I can think of a thousand different ways the money used to build a freaking ice bar could have paid rent or fed families or saved lives. My mom would be so pissed if she saw this kind of extravagance for a simple birthday party. And I can't say I'd disagree with her. I feel guilty just being here. But this is Hollywood, and this is the lifestyle of the rich and famous. And I'm here to party with Shrupty, so I push my resentment to the side and focus on making the most of it.

We skate slowly around the edge of the rink. Every now and then, the colorful lights hit her eyes and make them sparkle like diamonds. I can barely take my eyes off her, which is a problem considering I'm balancing precariously on two blades on top of slippery ice. Inevitably, I lose my balance, but she takes my hand and steadies me.

"You're doing great," she says, smiling at me. "I got you."

I smile back at her, and our gaze lingers as we move through the crowd. I'm falling for her. I'm falling so fast and so hard that it scares me.

And then I just fall. My skates give way, and I slide off my feet and onto my butt.

Shrupty gasps. "Are you okay?"

I sit up, trying to smile to cover up my embarrassment. "I'm fine."

She reaches a hand out to help me up, but she can only bend so far in that dress without flashing everyone at the party. I take her hand, but every time I try to stand, the skates slide out from under me again. People giggle at us as they zoom past. Shrupty presses her lips into a line, like she's trying to stifle her own laughter.

A part of me wants to cry, to crawl off the ice and run out of the party and never come back. But I don't have to let this get the best of me. As I sit on the freezing-cold rink, my butt damp, I realize I have a choice here: run from it or embrace the moment. I start to giggle, first just a little, but then Shrupty can't hold it in anymore either, and we both erupt in loud, overwhelming laughter.

"I'm stuck," I say. "Go on without me." We laugh even harder. Shrupty clutches her stomach in a fit of giggles, then loses her balance and drops to the floor next to me.

"Owww! Motherfucker!" she says, but she's still laughing.

We face each other, legs stretched out in front of us, hopelessly enjoying ourselves.

"I guess we live here now," I say.

She leans forward over her knees to tighten her laces. "I guess so."

People skate around us while we try pathetically to help each other up. My jeans are frozen to my butt cheeks, I can't stand up no matter how hard I try, and yet I don't remember the last time I had this much fun.

CHAPTER TWENTY

Eventually, people feel sorry enough for us to help us to our feet, and we slide off the ice and straight to the bar. I sit in a booth with a glass of water, while Shrupty waits at the bar to order us two of something called The Will—a signature drink created just for this party. According to the chalkboard menu behind the bar, it consists of blue Bombay Sapphire gin, Sprite, a twist of lime, a sprinkle of ginger, and a ton of ice cubes, topped with bright blue forget-me-not flowers. I wasn't planning to drink alcohol, but it's too beautiful not to at least taste it.

The song "Uptown Girl" comes on over the speakers, and I hum to it while I wait.

"Will you be my uptown girl?" a low voice mumbles in my ear, making me jump. Archer slides into the booth next to me, drink in hand.

"Oh, hey," I say. "Some party, huh?"

He shrugs. "I've been to better." This guy isn't impressed by much. I think he thinks it makes him seem laid-back and cool, but he just ends up looking obnoxious.

"You didn't answer my question, Uptown Girl," he says with a smirk.

I laugh through my discomfort. "There's nothing 'uptown' about my life."

"Come on," he says. "Don't act like Daddy didn't give you everything you wanted. I bet he even calls you 'princess.'"

That hits a sore spot for me, and I let him know it. "Listen, bud, you don't know anything about me."

He grins, like he's pleased to have made me mad. "We'll just have to do something about that, then. Come skate with me."

I shake my head. "I'm fine here, thanks."

"Come on," he says, reaching his hand out. "I'll be your downtown boy."

"No, thanks," I say. Then, because I'm still working on saying no assertively and feel like I need to lighten the mood: "I can't go on the ice with my drink anyway."

But that just makes it worse. He takes the glass of water from my hand and puts it on the table beside him.

"There," he says, smiling proudly. "Problem solved. Let's go."

He takes my hand and tries to take me with him, but I pull my hand back. "Hey! Can you not do that? I said no." Then I stand up, reach around him for my water, and start walking away. Some people nearby watch us with concern.

"Bex," he says as he follows me. "Chill, I'm not asking for much. Just one skate?"

I stop and turn around, ready to obliterate him. But more people turn to see what's going on, and I lose my courage. I walk over to a quiet corner and let him follow me so I can talk to him without causing a scene.

"Listen," I say. "I'm gay. Okay? *Gay.*"

His eyes widen. Then he looks me up and down, like he's searching for something. "You? Gay? No way."

"Um," I say, raising an eyebrow. "Yes way."

"Gay?"

"Gay."

"*Gay?*"

"GAY."

Archer is still looking at me like I'm a math equation he can't figure out. Then, with a sigh and a shrug, he gives up.

"Shame," he says. "We would've been great together."

I want to say something snarky, like "You wouldn't stand a chance with me if I wasn't gay, either." But coming out to him took a lot of energy, so I decide to change the subject instead.

"You're not drinking The Will?" I ask, gesturing to his glass of what looks like whiskey.

He makes a face like he's grossed out. "Nah. It's got flowers in it."

"So?"

"It's a girly drink."

"Um, beverages don't have a gender, my dude."

"Whatever." He takes a sip. "Here's a question: If you were a drink, what would you taste like?"

I ignore the way he waggles his eyebrows when he says *taste*.

"My signature drink would probably be sweet," I say. "I have a sweet tooth."

He winks at me. "I bet you do." He leans in closer, backing me against the ice-cold wall. "I'd be a hard liquor. Strong and powerful, like whiskey. Something that takes your breath away."

I put my hand on his chest and push him back gently. "You need to back up, man. I literally just told you, I'm gay. Like, super gay. And FYI, I've tried whiskey. I don't care for it."

He raises an eyebrow. "Maybe you just haven't tasted the right kind. Some are more mature than others."

"And others are just tacky," Shrupty says as she joins us. "Hyped up, watered down, and leave a bad taste in your mouth." I try to hide my smirk as Archer takes a step back, speechless.

"That's cold, Shrupty," he says. "I was just joking around."

"Well," she says to him, looking at his glass. "You better get a refill, Arch, because you're done."

He storms away, carrying his bruised ego back to the bar.

"Make sure to get extra ice for that burn," I call after him.

I give Shrupty a high five and we laugh like witches over a bubbling cauldron. I take a sip of my signature Will. I'm not a huge fan of the gin.

I push my glasses farther up my nose and turn to Shrupty. "What would your signature drink be?"

Shrupty taps her index finger on her chin as she thinks. "Hmm. Probably something like elderflower champagne. Have you ever had that?"

"Never even heard of it."

"It's popular at my aunt's restaurant. It's champagne, sugar, lemons, white wine vinegar, and elderflowers. It's sweet and flirty but has a bitterness to it that you don't expect. Just like me." She laughs. "What about you?"

"I really don't know enough about alcohol to decide," I say. "But probably something with a ton of sugar in it."

Shrupty moves closer to me, her fingers brushing against my hip. "You don't have to finish that drink if it's too much for you. I'm, like, a hundred percent sure it's ninety-nine percent alcohol."

I immediately recoil and place the glass on the table. "Yeah, I'm not playing with that."

Shrupty giggles. "Your signature drink would definitely be a virgin."

I avoid eye contact with her. My skin runs hot enough to melt the whole damn ice bar. Seeing my reaction, Shrupty's eyes widen, and so does her smile.

She leans in, her lips brushing against my ear, and whispers, "You're so cute when you're embarrassed."

I try to laugh, but it gets caught in my throat and emerges as a weird sputter. "Well," I say, coughing. "Good thing embarrassment is my default setting."

Shrupty dips her chin, and when she speaks, her voice is low. "Good thing."

A high-pitched voice interrupts our flirting.

"Oh my god. *Shrup*?"

An athletic blonde with an entourage approaches.

"Erica? Hey!" Shrupty seems happy to see her, giving her a quick hug.

"How are you?" Erica asks, tracing her hands down Shrupty's arms. "It's been ages." Erica looks familiar, but I can't put my finger on where I've seen her before. She has to be at least six feet tall, with long wavy hair and pouty lips—perhaps she's a model.

Her entourage shuffles her away, mumbling about mingling and networking. When Shrupty turns back to me, she puffs her cheeks up and blows out a long sigh, like she's relieved.

"Sorry," she says. "I would have introduced you, but she's always rolling in and out of places like a hurricane."

"Is she on TV or something?" I ask. "I know her face."

"She's done a bit of everything," she says. "TV, film, music . . . She's very versatile like that. Her dad is a huge movie producer."

"Wow. How do you know her?"

"We went to high school together." She smiles fondly at a memory. "We actually went to prom together. She was prom queen and I was prom king. That was before they stopped gendering it. After graduation we hung out a couple of times. But we never really got serious."

"How come?" I ask, then wonder if I'm prying too much. "I mean, if you don't mind me asking."

"It's fine," she says. "We just couldn't make it work. She was always rushing off to the next job or party or whatever. And whenever we did get time alone, Erica just had this wall up. She'd been burned so many times by jerks who used her for her money or connections. She wouldn't let herself open up to anyone. Which is totally fair—I've been burned before, too. It sucks to find out someone you thought cared about you was just using you for their own agenda. But that's one of the downsides of LA: Everyone is looking out for number one."

My shoulders slump, and I think of Malcolm. "I've noticed that."

She frowns. "Oh no. I hope you haven't been screwed over already!"

"Eh," I say with a shrug. "Nothing I can't handle."

"Did you go to your prom?" she asks.

I gulp down my drink, trying to ignore the taste. "Yeah," I lie. It's easier that way. If I say no, she'll ask why and I'll have to tell her that Emily Rose threatened to beat me up if I showed my face at prom, and that even if I'd wanted to go, I wouldn't have been able to afford a suit anyway. And even if I could have afforded a suit, it would've just led to a conversation with my mom I wasn't ready for. She'd ask why I wasn't wearing a pretty dress; I'd say I feel more comfortable in suits. Then I'd have to avoid divulging anything more—partly out of fear of her realizing I'm gay, partly because I'm still firmly in the questioning category when it comes to my gender identity. And, ugh, that whole scenario is exhausting just to think about.

"What was your prom night like?" she asks.

I swallow hard. "It was great. How about yours?"

She grins. "Same. The whole night was a blast. In fact, high school was a blast for me. I know it wasn't that long ago, but I miss it. Those were the best days of my life."

"Wow," I say, not even trying to hide my surprise. "Really?"

Shrupty chuckles. "Is that weird?"

Yes. "No." I shrug. "I've just never met anyone who actually enjoyed high school before."

"Maybe I'm weird. I mean, yeah, there were jerks. This one girl refused to say my name right for the whole of freshman year—she kept calling me Shifty."

I make a face. "That's horrible."

"Yeah," she says. "I hated her. But I still loved going to school, hanging with friends, being on the cheer squad. I miss it a little." She pouts, her bottom lip sticking out in the most adorable way. "You don't miss hanging out with your friends at lunch?"

My stomach flips nervously. I need to change the subject. "Yeah, I guess. Ready to hit the ice again?"

She nods, and a minute later we're stepping back onto the ice. Please, O mighty ice-skating gods, don't let me fall again. I take two awkward, slippery steps before I lose my footing and fall backward. Luckily, Shrupty is right behind me and catches me before I hit the ground. Somehow, I manage to spin around so I'm facing her, and she takes my hands to steady me.

"Is this okay?" she asks, squeezing my fingers between hers.

I nod. "Don't let go."

She smiles. "I won't."

She starts skating backward like she's Adam freaking Rippon, gently guiding me around the edge of the rink. The DJ starts playing Janelle Monáe's "Make Me Feel," and Shrupty starts singing along. And because she wasn't already incredible enough, her voice sounds amazing. Smooth as velvet, just like her hands as they hold mine. Our eyes meet as she sings the words, and I don't let myself look away. Warmth spreads through my whole body; the heat between us is enough to turn the ice into a lake. She strokes the back of my hand with her thumb and it sends goose bumps rippling over my skin.

I swallow my nerves and tell her something I've wanted to say since the day we met. "You're so pretty."

The corner of her mouth lifts into an adorable half smile. "Thank you. So are you."

My heart sprouts wings and flutters around in my chest. Our skating slows to a halt, and we're standing so close now that I can feel her chest rise against mine with every breath.

"Come a little closer," she says. I inch forward, our bodies pressed against each other.

She touches her hand to her neck absentmindedly but then gasps. "Oh no. No, no, no, no, no." She backs away, her head darting around like she's looking for something.

"Are you okay?" I ask. I try to follow her as she skates away, but there's only so far I can go without losing my balance.

"No," she says, her voice high. "I lost my necklace! Do you see it?"

I scan the area, but it's impossible to see much in the dim lighting and with so many people darting around us. "We'll find it."

But we don't. We skate around for fifteen minutes. Well, she skates; I struggle along the railed edge. Charlie and Alyssa even join the hunt, using the flashlights on their phones to help. With each second that passes, Shrupty grows more and more upset. She skates over to me with tears in her eyes and her hand clutching her chest.

"It's gone," she says. "My grandmother's necklace is gone. My mom is going to murder me." She speeds away again in a panic.

I mentally retrace our steps and glance over to the place where we fell earlier, squinting at the ice through the swirling lights. Something sparkly catches the light for a split second, and I know I've found it.

"Shrupty!" I call, but she's too far away and the music is too loud for her to hear me. Taking matters into my own hands, I slowly skate over to it. The silver chain and emerald pendant are almost invisible against the ice, but when the reflections of the disco ball hit it just right, it glows like it's calling her name. I bend down to pick it up, and once again I fall onto my butt. But I have the necklace, safe in my hand, and that's all that matters.

"Shrupty!" I call again, waving my arm frantically to get her attention. Finally, she sees me, and I let the necklace hang from my fingers. Her face lights up, and she skates over so fast I worry she's going to ride right over me.

"You found it!" she gasps as she falls to her knees at my side. "Oh my god." She takes it from my hands and inspects it, then smiles as tears run down her cheeks. "Thank you, thank you, thank you."

She clasps the necklace back around her neck, then leans closer and pulls me into a hug. I run my hand through her soft hair, suddenly feeling like we're the only people on the rink. Shrupty leans back just enough to look at me, our noses almost touching. I want so desperately to kiss her, but I'm frozen.

Her gaze flickers to my mouth and then back to my eyes, and I know she's thinking the same thing.

"Can I kiss you?" I ask. My voice is so quiet, there's no way she could hear it over the music, but she must know what I'm asking, because she smiles. And then she leans in, and my eyes close naturally. Her lips meet mine, and she cups my face in her hands, her fingers cold against my cheeks. All I want to do is drag her away from the party and take her somewhere private and warm, somewhere we can stay like this all night.

CHAPTER TWENTY-ONE

Later, Shrupty and I walk out of the party and into what looks like the aftermath of a fight.

One of the bouncers holds ice up to his cheekbone, and an ambulance is backing into the alleyway, red lights flashing silently.

We walk through the gap in the fence to find Archer on the other side of the alley, stretched out on the ground next to a puddle of vomit. Two paramedics climb out of the ambulance and hurry over to him. Shrupty and I stand out of their way as they kneel beside Archer.

"How you feeling, buddy?" one of the medics asks.

Archer doesn't respond. More people filter out of the party to see what's going on. The medics take Archer's arms, trying to lift him up into a seated position. Suddenly, Archer starts thrashing around like a toddler who doesn't want to be disciplined and falls back to the ground with a thud.

"Fuck off!" he yells. "I said fuck off!"

A girl standing next to me takes her phone out and starts filming. I glance around the growing crowd and see another five or six phones held in the air. This is not good.

Archer groans and pushes a hand through his hair, and I notice red marks on his knuckles. He must have punched that bouncer. What a dick.

One of the paramedics crouches down again and puts a hand on Archer's shoulder. "Listen, bro," he says. "We're just trying to help you out. Let's get you to sit up, okay?"

He reaches down to try to help Archer up one more time, but Archer just swats his hands away.

"What are you, gay?" Archer spits, staring at the paramedic with his nose scrunched up. "Quit touching me."

And suddenly, a party that was supposed to be a safe space feels the exact opposite. I feel a pit form in my gut. My skin starts to prickle and I break into a sweat. Shrupty stiffens beside me, her jaw clenched and gaze glued to Archer like she's cussing him out in her mind. I look around and see dozens of horrified faces. But everyone here who's queer? They just look tired. Tired of that kind of shit. *Done.*

The paramedic stops moving, like he's shocked. "What did you just say to me?"

Archer waves his hands in front of him wildly. "Fuck, everyone is gay now. This whole party is the gayest fucking thing I've ever seen!" He finally notices the people loitering in the alley, watching him, then turns his anger on all of us. "What about me? Huh? What about straight people?" He raises a fist in the air. "Straight pride!"

My jaw drops. Scoffs and groans rumble through the crowd. Someone behind me mutters, "You've got to be fucking kidding me."

But Archer isn't deterred, and goes on like that for longer than anyone wants him to. His lightly veiled homophobia is peeking out from behind the curtains. With every word he says, I deflate a little more. It's just another reminder that *oh*, right, I'm different. Oh, right. There are some places where I'm not welcome. Oh, right. Even people I think I can trust would prefer it if I just didn't exist.

I catch sight of Will and Ryan standing on the other side of the fence, apologizing to the bouncers. They must be able to hear Archer's ranting, because Will stops and turns to listen. Then his head falls in disappointment, and I feel terrible for him. Archer is supposed to be his friend, his castmate of six years. I can't stay quiet.

"Hey," I call to Archer, trying to sound as angry as I feel. "That's enough."

He searches the crowd for whoever is yelling at him, and I freeze up. What if he outs me to everyone here? What if he starts throwing insults—or punches—in my direction? But to my relief, he's much too drunk to figure out it was me. Phew.

Ryan, Will's boyfriend and host of the party, comes to the

rescue. "Arch, man. We get it. Everyone's gay, this party is gay, and you're wasted. Now let the nice paramedics do their jobs so you can go home and sleep it off, yeah?"

Archer looks up at Ryan, and I hold my breath. My hand finds Shrupty's beside me, and I squeeze it tight. My anxious brain goes into danger mode. I locate the nearest exits. Take note of how far the bouncers are from Ryan. If something happened, it would only take a couple of seconds for them to step in. The medics are already here, so if anyone gets hurt they'll be assisted right away. My mind is on high alert and my body is braced and ready to run. I've seen how these things play out too many times before.

Fights broke out at school or in the parking lot at Sonic every week, and they got vicious fast. One minute two guys are getting up in each other's business, the next there's twenty dudes throwing punches and people lying bleeding on the ground. If this goes south, my only priority is to get Shrupty and myself out of here as fast and as safely as possible.

But all my worry is over nothing. Archer hangs his head in shame, then finally lets the paramedics help him to his feet. As they lead him to the back of the open ambulance, he looks around the crowd of people watching him and frowns.

"I'm sorry," he says quietly. "I didn't mean it. Just ignore me. Everyone else does."

Exasperated sighs echo around me.

"No one feels sorry for you, Mr. Straight White TV Star,"

someone calls out. People laugh. I'm still trying to breathe through my brief moment of panic.

The crowd starts to disperse, and Shrupty and I walk around the ambulance and toward the street. Some girls behind us talk about how their videos of Archer are going to go viral. Someone I don't know suggests selling it to TMZ.

"This is going to cause some trouble on Monday," I say to Shrupty.

She nods. "I know. As if I wasn't nervous enough about my first day. Now I gotta work with a homophobe." She sighs and rests her head on my shoulder while we wait for our Uber. Having her next to me melts away some of my anxiety. I kiss the top of her head, hoping it will comfort her like she's comforting me.

"Are you cold?" she asks randomly. It's summer in LA, and I'm practically sweating through my shirt.

"Nope. Why?"

She runs a hand down my arm. "You're shaking."

I look down at my arms. They're covered in goose bumps where she just touched me. "I'm just shaken up from the fight." I close my eyes because I'm just so exhausted by myself sometimes. "I thought Archer was about to take a shot at Ryan. And then Ryan would have fought back and others would have jumped in and before we knew what was happening we would have been stuck in the middle of a rumble."

Shrupty giggles. "A rumble? Are you from, like, *West Side Story* or something?"

I laugh with her. "Something like that."

"We were fine," she adds. "Guys like Archer and Ryan don't fight. At least, not like *that*. Besides, Arch couldn't even stand up by himself. No way would he have tried it, especially not with Ry. His muscles have muscles."

"Are you all right?" I ask.

She gives me a sideways glance and says, "Please, I saw through that dude's performative allyship years ago, before I even met him. I have zero fucks to give about what he thinks."

Our car pulls up, and we climb inside. She holds my hand as the car rolls out of the neighborhood and back toward the city.

"Wanna come to my place tomorrow?" she asks, her head resting on the seat. "Help me rehearse my lines?"

I smile at her. "Definitely."

CHAPTER TWENTY-TWO

The next morning, I'm on the bus to Shrupty's house, giddy with excitement that I get to see her again. But as we roll through the gates of her neighborhood, that excitement turns to nervousness. My face is practically pressed up to the window as I see one mansion after another, each bigger than the next. There are sprawling compounds, protected by tall steel gates. Three- and four-story homes adorned with Roman-style pillars and elaborate fountains and surrounded by palm trees. With every multimillion-dollar house I see, the voice in my head whispering *you don't belong here* grows louder and louder. I glance down at my ripped jeans, scuffed sneakers, and faded white tee that used to be my mom's. Am I underdressed to even set foot in this suburb? I wanted to ask Parker for a quick makeup and hair session, but he stayed at Dante's last night, and I'd never touch his brushes without supervision.

I step off the bus and use Google Maps on my phone to

guide me to Shrupty's house. Then I stare up at it for a minute in awe, like I'm staring at a painting in an art gallery. It's a wide, two-story mansion, with a dozen windows, two chimneys, and an arched driveway surrounded by a manicured rose garden, all behind a white gate with the house number on it in cursive.

"It's a goddamn palace," I whisper. I look up at the gate, trying to figure out how to get inside. Then I notice an intercom on the left-side wall and press the button with the symbol of a bell on it.

"Hello?" Shrupty's voice comes through the speaker, making me smile.

"Hey!" I say. "It's me, uh, Bex. Permission to come aboard?"

I hear her laugh; then there's a loud buzz and the gates start to swing open. My hands shake with nerves, so I tug my shirt down, double-check the zipper of my jeans, then pull them up a little higher, push my glasses farther up my nose, anything to keep myself busy and burn off some of my anxious energy.

Shrupty opens the door as I walk up to the porch, and when I see her I almost trip on the last step. She's glowing, wearing athletic leggings and a purple sports bra. Her abs glisten with sweat.

"Hey!" she says. "I won't hug you because I just finished with my trainer, but come in!"

The thing about being gay is that when I'm attracted to a girl it's sometimes difficult to tell if I want her body or if I . . .

ahem . . . *want* her body. Like, am I jealous of her abs, or am I turned on by her abs? Is it both? My abs are hidden under softness, a belly that I will probably always have because I loathe working out. I'm cool with that. So in this instance, it's not jealousy I'm feeling but attraction. Intense, overwhelming, burning attraction that clouds my mind . . . and obviously takes my breath away because suddenly I realize I haven't said a word since I arrived on her doorstep.

"Hi!" I blurt out, much too late. She giggles, then turns and walks down the hall. I try to look literally anywhere else but at her butt, and that's when I notice the inside of her castle . . . er, I mean, home.

I'm standing in an open foyer, with clean white floors and a staircase on each side leading to the second floor. A glass table sits proudly in the center, adorned with white roses in a crystal vase. A chandelier hangs above it from the high ceiling, sparkling in the sunlight coming through the upstairs windows.

Shrupty glances down at my shoes. "Um, do you mind taking your shoes off? My parents have a thing about shoes in the house."

"Oh, sure," I say. My pulse quickens. She's going to see my old socks with holes in the soles. I quickly slip my shoes off and leave them beside the door, my anxiety rising.

"The front door is ajar," a feminine robot voice says, making me squeal in fright.

"What the fuck was that?" I ask, looking above me. "Did your house just *talk* to me?"

Shrupty laughs at me from the end of the hall. "Yeah. Just nudge the door and it will close by itself."

I turn to the door, poke it with my index finger just enough for it to move, and it swings closed just like she said it would. "Jesus," I whisper to myself. "This is *rich*."

"You can come inside, you know," Shrupty calls, waving me over.

I thought I *was* inside. How big is this place? I hurry down the hall to catch up with her, thinking of my mom and how she would die if she were here. Shrupty leads me into a spacious kitchen and living area, with floor-to-ceiling windows that flood the room with light. She opens the fridge and takes out a bottle of water.

"Can I get you anything?" she asks.

I shake my head, still taking everything in. "I'm good."

A kid with long, gangly arms, shaggy black hair, and what looks like his first attempt to grow a mustache sits at the kitchen counter, eating a bowl of Froot Loops. He glances up at me before returning his attention to his phone.

"Who's the white girl?" he asks, like he's bored with me already.

Shrupty takes a sip of water, then gestures to me. "Ajay, this is Bex. Bex, this is my brother, Ajay."

I smile and give him a quick wave. He doesn't react. A woman's voice calls Shrupty's name from somewhere else in the house.

"I'm busy, Mom!" Shrupty calls back. That seems to displease her mom, because the next thing I hear is her yelling something in another language. Shrupty yells back, then sighs and turns to me. "Be right back."

Suddenly I'm standing alone in the kitchen with Shrupty's little brother, who won't stop staring at me.

"You're allowed to sit down, you know," he says.

I don't know where Shrupty wants to rehearse, so I decide to wait. "I'm good, thanks. I'll just wait for Shrupty."

He narrows his eyes at me. "Are you her new girlfriend?"

"What?" I ask. "No." My cheeks burn. My gaze drops to the spotless white floor.

"Then why are you blushing?" he asks with a smirk. "I know she has a girlfriend. You don't have to lie. It's not a big deal."

"I'm not lying," I say, but something he said makes me curious. "How do you know she has a girlfriend?"

He sticks his tongue out like he's grossed out. "She's been walking around the house singing Carly Rae Jepsen like she always does when she starts dating someone. It's annoying."

Just then, Shrupty returns. "Jay! Stop harassing our guest."

A mischievous grin spreads across his face, and he launches into the chorus of "Call Me Maybe." I can't help it, I giggle.

Shrupty gives him a smug look, then says something to him in another language. My name comes up, but other than that I have no idea what she's saying. His eyes widen, and he drops his spoon into his bowl. Then Shrupty takes my hand and pulls me out of the kitchen.

"Were you speaking Hindi?" I ask, and she shakes her head.

"Marathi," she says.

"Oh, sorry," I say. "What did you say to him? He looked terrified."

She grins. "I said that if he's not nice to you, I'd tell Mom and Dad about the time he borrowed my iPad and forgot to delete his search history."

I laugh as she leads me up the stairs.

CHAPTER TWENTY-THREE

"Whoa," I say as I look around Shrupty's bedroom. "This is your room?"

"Yep," she says casually as she steps into her walk-in closet, which is bigger than Parker's living room. I'm about to follow her, but she starts lifting her sports bra up to take it off, and I spin around and look out her window instead. Just then, my phone buzzes with a notification from *Entertainment Now*: "Archer Carlton Apologizes for Homophobic Rant."

I've purposefully been avoiding social media this morning, not wanting to relive the hurt and fear I felt in that alleyway. But I guess those amateur paparazzi videos at the party went viral just like they said they would.

"Oh my god," I say. "Archer released a statement."

Shrupty scoffs from inside her walk-in. "You mean his PR team released a statement. What does it say?"

I clear my throat and start reading it aloud.

"'I am deeply embarrassed by my drunken behavior. I meant no offense, and I apologize if my poor attempt at humor was misinterpreted. I do not have a homophobic bone in my body. The words I chose to use in that private moment caught on video are regrettable. My true friends and fans will see that this one brief, drunken moment does not represent the totality of who I am or what I believe.'"

Shrupty walks out, and she and I stare at each other, swapping looks that say "Are you fucking kidding me."

"And the award for best celebrity non-apology goes to . . . ," she says.

I laugh, then notice the old T-shirt she's wearing and gasp.

"Is that a *Twilight* T-shirt?" I ask, unashamedly enthusiastic.

She looks down at her baggy black shirt with CULLEN BASEBALL TEAM 2008 on it. "Haha, yeah. I was obsessed with it."

I clutch my heart with my hands. "Oh my god, same! Parker and I went to every midnight screening."

Shrupty grins. "My friends and I waited outside the Nokia Theatre alllllll damn day for the premiere of *Breaking Dawn: Part Two*."

I gasp. "You went to the premiere?"

"Not as, like, VIPs or anything," she says. "We were in the crowd outside. But I did get to meet Kristen Stewart, so that was awesome."

I'm going to die of jealousy right here in her room. "Did she talk to you? What was she like? Did she smell good?"

Shrupty laughs. "She was very sweet. Here." She pulls one of the photos off her wall and hands it to me. It's tween Shrupty, wearing a baby blue dress and grinning at the camera. Kristen Stewart is crouching down next to her, wearing a nude strapless gown and giving her trademark half smile.

"I'm so jealous," I say. "You have no idea."

Shrupty smiles as she looks at the photo. "Aww, I was such a little Twi-hard." She sticks the picture back on her wall, and I step closer to see the dozens of others around it. There are photos of her from her high school days with her friends, sitting around the lunch table in their uniforms and making faces. Others show her at different concerts, her face decorated with glitter as bands play in the background. Vacation memories from Rome, Paris, New York, Sydney, and all kinds of tropical islands. I see her with famous faces; Mix Chloe, the gang from the Brightsiders, and Alyssa and Charlie. A Halloween photo from when she was about five or six, dressed as Hermione Granger. It's a collage of her life, and with every photo I see I feel myself falling for her even more.

Shrupty points to some recent Polaroids of her wearing a stunning pink-and-gold sari.

"That was at my cousin's wedding last year in India," she says. "It was amazing."

An older couple stand on either side of her. "Are they your parents?"

Shrupty smiles. "Yeah. They've got their serious faces on in that photo, but they're really just giant goofballs. They were born in Mumbai and came here after they got married, but we go back to visit about once a year." Then she opens the sliding door onto her balcony. "Alexa, play 'Shrupty's Good Vibes Only Playlist.'"

Music fills the room, coming from speakers in the ceiling. I try to hide how impressed I am by her house, because to her this is all totally normal. For me, it's like stepping into everything I've always dreamed about.

"Come outside," she says as she stretches out on a wide rainbow-striped hammock. I step out onto the balcony, overwhelmed by the luxury of it all. The backyard is lush and green, with a sparkling swimming pool in the center, a pool house to the left, and a cabana lounge on the right.

"Wow," I say quietly as I take it all in. "You must throw some pretty epic pool parties here."

Shrupty laughs. "Yeah. But my friend Luke's parents installed a hot tub our junior year, so we mostly hung out there." She sits up and crosses her legs. "What about you? Was your house the party house for your friends?"

"Ummm," I say, stalling. The closest I ever came to going to a house party was going to Gabby's mom's surprise fiftieth birthday party. And I was only invited so Gabby didn't have to spend the whole night listening to her aunties bickering. We stole a bottle of champagne and sat on the roof drinking it and talking about *Silver Falls*. I smile at the memory, then get hit with something I've never felt before. Homesickness.

"Bex?" Shrupty says, still waiting for my answer.

"Nah," I say quickly. "Should we start going over your lines?" I get my backpack from her bed and take the script out. When I step back outside, she's watching me closely. I feel her eyes on me as I wriggle in next to her on the hammock.

"Parker said you guys lived together, right?" she asks. "Growing up?"

"Yeah," I say. "Which scene do you want to start with?"

She's quiet for a moment. I flip open the script and pretend I'm deeply interested in what I'm reading. In the back of my mind, I can hear Parker's voice. *I'm not embarrassed or ashamed about how we grew up . . . And you shouldn't be either.*

I'm not ashamed . . . I'm just protective. People can be judgmental assholes, and I want Shrupty to get to know me for who I am, not for where I'm from.

Ugh. It's getting harder to convince myself that *that's* really why I've been avoiding talking about home with her. Especially because Shrupty is probably the least judgmental person I've ever met.

She reaches out for me, walking her fingers over my hand

and up my arm. I forget everything I was worrying about just a second earlier.

"Will you take a photo of me with the script?" she asks. I nod.

She lays back on the hammock, holding the script open in front of her and pretending she's reading intently, her brow furrowed in concentration. I snap a couple dozen pics from different angles, then give her phone back, and she starts going through to find the best ones.

"Remember to block out the episode title," I say. "Don't wanna give away too many spoilers."

After running the photo through some filters, she adds a rainbow and the emoji of two girls holding hands to the picture, then blasts it all over her social media. I open all my apps so I can retweet, regram, and reblog it everywhere.

We lay next to each other on the hammock, both scrolling on our phones to read all the reactions flowing in.

"Someone just asked if I'm playing a queer character," she says with a smile. "Should I say yes?"

I press my lips into a line, thinking. "Hmm. Maybe hint at it? I don't know how much you're allowed to reveal."

She nods, then retweets the fan question with a winking-face emoji next to a pride flag. "The gays are going to love this."

We laugh, then she lifts her hand to my temple and strokes my hair back.

"I like your freckles," she says. She starts lightly touching each freckle, connecting them like a dot-to-dot over my cheek, then boops my nose. "You're really pretty, do you know that?"

I can't wipe the smile off my face. "Thanks."

She tilts her head to the side and puts on a high-pitched voice. "So you agree? You think you're really pretty." Then she starts laughing at her own joke, and I'm smitten. "*Mean Girls* is one of my favorite movies, FYI."

"My birthday is October third," I say, smiling proudly. Being born on *Mean Girls* day is one fact about myself that I'm always ready to whip out whenever someone brings up the movie. Or the musical. Or Lindsay Lohan.

Shrupty's mouth falls open. "Get out! Seriously?"

"Yep! It's pretty much the only cool thing about me. I'm very proud of it."

She laughs. "You should be. But I wouldn't say it's the only cool thing about you. I can think of at least ten other things right now. You're kind of wonderful, Bex Phillips."

Her fingers reach my shoulder, sending a shiver down my spine. My gaze falls to her lips, the same lips I kissed on the ice twelve hours earlier. The lips I dreamed about all night long.

As though sensing my thoughts, she bites her bottom lip. It drives me wild. I swallow hard, then lean in and crush my mouth to hers. She kisses me back like she's been waiting for me to do that ever since I walked through her front door.

The script falls from my lap and onto the floor, but I hardly notice. I feel her leaning back, relaxing into the hammock. She clutches the neckline of my shirt in her hand, pulling me down with her until I'm on top of her. My hands run down her sides, stopping at her hips. Our tongues meld together, and she wraps her arms around my neck, pinning me to her. I feel like the whole world is shifting on its axis, but it's just the hammock swinging as we move together.

Shrupty moans as we kiss, and my temperature rises tenfold at the sound. I need to pause for air, but if I had to choose between breathing and kissing her, I'd choose this kiss every single time. I'm lost in her.

"Shruptyyy!" a voice calls from inside the house. I reluctantly pull myself away from her.

"Did you hear that?" I ask.

She pouts, like she's sad that I stopped kissing her. "Hear what?"

"Shrupty!" her mom calls again; this time she sounds closer.

Shrupty gasps. "My mom's coming."

We scramble to climb off the hammock, but it keeps swinging wildly every time we move. I manage to crawl off her, and she slides off the side. But the kickback from her getting off the hammock is stronger than I expected, and next thing I know I've rolled off and hit the floor with a thud.

"Shit," Shrupty says. "Are you okay?"

I'm lying under the hammock, arching my sore back.

"Fine," I croak. I lift my hand in the air to give her a thumbs-up.

Just then, I hear her bedroom door open.

"There you are," her mom says. "Didn't you hear me calling you?"

Shrupty stands in the doorway to her balcony, tugging her shirt down. "Sorry, Ma." She waves for me to come over, so I climb to my feet.

"This is my new friend," Shrupty says as I stand next to her. "Bex."

Her mom smiles. Shrupty looks just like her. Her dark brown hair is streaked with silver at the front, and she's wearing a sky blue caftan with yellow trim and matching pants.

"Oh, hello, Bex. Good to meet you," she says.

"You too," I say as I rub the back of my neck self-consciously.

They start talking in Marathi, then her mom leaves and Shrupty turns to me. "I just need to help my mom for a sec. She wants me to help her post some pics to Facebook for my aunties before she goes to work."

"Where does she work?" I ask.

"She's an ob-gyn at Cedars Sinai." She smiles proudly. "She delivers all the celebrity babies."

"Wow, that's so cool," I say. After she leaves, I go back out onto the hammock and lie down, replaying our kiss over and over again.

CHAPTER TWENTY-FOUR

I arrive to work the next day to find out the writers' room has been canceled.

"Who knows," Jane says when I ask why. "Angela is down at the reception desk, so he's not with her." She scoops up her folder from her desk and I carry her bag and her coffee as we walk down the hall. "I am really running out of patience with that man."

Jane seems more openly frustrated with him every day. It's understandable; she's been working with him since he was hired three years ago. To be honest, I'm surprised it took this long for the cracks to start showing. There's a sinking feeling in my gut, telling me that it's only a matter of time before this blows up.

People have limits, and I can see by the near-constant anger in Jane's eyes that she's bubbling closer and closer to hers. I just hope I'm there to see it when she does. Malcolm's time is running out.

We speed-walk to the set, and the whole time Jane is rattling off all the things on her very impressive to-do list. After she pauses to take a breath, she sighs, then turns to me. "Are you sure you want to do my job one day?"

I grin and nod. "More than anything."

She chuckles. "Ah, you're a masochist. Just like me."

"I guess so," I say, laughing with her.

When we walk through the double doors and onto the set, the tension is palpable. Then I notice Archer and Will arguing by the door of the cabin.

"Didn't you see my apology, man?" Archer asks.

Will rolls his eyes. "Yeah, I saw it. But I wouldn't exactly call it an apology."

Archer throws his arms up in the air. "I've been catching so much heat for this. I don't know what anyone wants me to say."

"Jesus, Arch," Will says. He has bags under his eyes, like he hasn't slept in days. "Did you ever think that maybe this isn't about you?"

Archer snaps back, "Tell that to the thousands of people online telling me to kill myself."

"I'm sorry," Will says. "That's never okay."

"No," Archer says, crossing his arms. "And it's all because I made some stupid comment about being straight. Do you know what it feels like to be harassed over something like that?"

Will gives him a harsh stare. "Yes. Yes, I fucking do."

Realizing his mistake, Archer sighs. "Yeah. Okay. Fair point."

Even from the other side of the set, I can see Will's nostrils flare in anger. "I'm done trying to help you understand." Then he walks away, leaving Archer standing alone. Archer punches the thin wood of the set wall, putting his hand right through it. Startled, my breath catches in my throat.

Jane groans. "Great. The last thing we need right now is feuding talent and holes in the fucking walls." She falls into her chair and starts rubbing her temples. "I'm getting a headache."

"I'll get you some water," I say.

"And a bagel," she adds. "Please."

. . .

Later, I'm on my way to the editing bay to watch clips from last week's episode shoot with Jane, when Shrupty marches toward me out of nowhere.

"Hey," I say with a smile. "How's your first official day going?" But then I notice the expression on her face. She's clenching her jaw so tight she could shatter her teeth, and the script in her hand is practically crushed into a ball.

She throws it at me like it's trash. "What the hell are you playing at with this?"

"Whoa," I say, stunned by her anger. "What's happening?"

She glares at me, hands on hips. "These new pages are bullshit. How could you do this?"

I pick up the script and try to flatten it out so I can read it. "New pages?"

I flip open to the new scenes, and my jaw falls open. No wonder she threw it like it was trash—it is.

INT. TOM'S HOUSE—NIGHT

Tom enters. He turns on a lamp, walks into the kitchen, and opens the fridge for a beer. A shadow moves past in the background that he doesn't see. He closes the fridge, walks back into the living room, sips the beer, and puts it on the coffee table. Then he spins around and pushes the intruder against the wall, holding his knife to their throat.

TOM

You have to do a lot better than that to fool me, hunter.

Lyla smiles at him.

```
And you have to do a lot better
than that to scare me, dog.
```

I look up at Shrupty. "Wait. *Tom* and Lyla? Where's Sasha?"

"That's what I want to know," she snaps, crossing her arms over her chest. "How could you rewrite my whole character without telling me? And to change her sexuality and hook her up with fucking Archer 'Straight Pride' Carlton? That's low."

"I'm just as mad as you are," I say, but she rolls her eyes.

"Bex, your name is on the front. Don't lie to me."

I flip the script to the front, and she's right.

WRITTEN BY MALCOLM BUTLER AND BEX PHILLIPS

You've got to be kidding me. I finally get my writing credit, only now I don't want my name anywhere near this garbage.

"Was this the plan all along?" she asks. "Make up some story about a groundbreaking queer story line on a historically heteronormative show, then flip the script the second I show up on set and it's too late to back out?"

"What? No! I don't—"

Her arms fall by her sides, and her scowl turns into a frown. She glances around to make sure no one is listening, then leans in close. "Do you even like me?"

"Shrupty," I say, looking her straight in the eyes. "Yes. I do. I like you, a lot."

"Then why don't I know anything about you?" she asks as she backs away. "You always change the subject if I ask about your life. You deflect or give one-word answers or *kick your cousin* under the table."

My heart sinks with shame. "You knew about that?"

She rolls her eyes. "I was right there, Bex." She buries her face in her hands. "Fuck. All these red flags. You don't care about me, you just wanted to use me for the show."

"No!" I try to explain, but it's hard when I don't know what's happening myself.

Dirk walks over then. "Shrupty, they're ready for you on set."

"Thanks," Shrupty says with a sad smile. "I'll be right there."

Dirk sees the new pages and turns to me. "Sorry it took me so long to add your credit." He smiles, but it's pure evil. "Good work on the rewrites."

He walks away, and I'm completely lost for words. That motherfucking asshole. Shrupty turns to me with tears in her eyes.

"Do you know how many times this town has tried to change me? When I started my YouTube channel, people said I should focus more on my beauty tutorials and tone down my political talk. I said no. When my videos started going viral, people said I should change my name to something that makes white people more comfortable. I said no." She shakes her head.

"Now, I finally put my trust in someone to tell a story I can be proud of, and you do this?"

Her shoulders hunch, and she closes her eyes. "I'm so tired of people trying to erase who I am." Then she looks at me like I've ripped her heart out, and I feel my own heart break. "I can't believe I trusted you. I can't believe I was falling for you."

My head spins as she leaves me standing alone, wishing more than anything that I could take all of her pain away. How did this happen?

I open the script again. The more I read, the more furious I get. Malcolm swapped Archer's character, Tom, with Alyssa's character, Sasha. In this version of the episode, Lyla swoons all over Tom and they hook up. She doesn't even have one scene with Sasha. He erased her queerness completely.

I march off set and through the lot, the pages crumpling in my fists. When I reach Malcolm's office, he's sitting in his chair by the window, scrolling on his phone. I throw the script onto the desk in front of him and ask him the question that keeps racing through my mind.

"Why?"

He looks up at me, eyebrows pinched. "Don't start."

"Why did you rewrite Lyla?" I ask, pointing at the wrinkled papers of the episode.

He groans. "I knew you were going to make this into a thing."

"You're damn right I am," I say. "There's no reason to do

this. The episode was perfect the way it was. It was going to change the whole show."

"Stop busting my balls," he says. "You must've heard what happened over the weekend. Archer is the star of this show; what he says and does reflects on us. If people love him, they love us. If they hate him, they hate us. And wow, do they hate us right now." He leans forward, tapping his pen on his desk. "I had to give him a softer story line. Something to make viewers fall in love with him again, trust him again. And nothing's softer than a romance."

"Wait," I say, resting my palms on the desk. "*That's* why you did this? To repair his reputation? This is all about optics."

He shrugs nonchalantly. "That, and Archer and Will need some time to cool off. Archer has already been up here whining about Will's attitude this morning."

"Yeah," I say. "Will's pissed. And he has every right to be."

"Whatever," he says. "I'm not debating this with you. The rewrite stays."

"So you're going to punish everyone else for Archer's mistake? Everyone else has to suffer just to make a homophobe feel better?"

"Who's suffering?" he asks, looking around the room. "This is a fucking television show, for Christ's sake. Why do you care so much?"

"Because I am Lyla!" I shout. "And Shrupty is Lyla. Alyssa is Lyla and thousands of *Silver Falls* fans are Lyla. By doing this, you are telling them that they don't matter. That they can be erased and no one will care. Well, I care. And I'm not going to let you do this."

Malcolm tilts his head to the side and examines me. "You're gay?"

"Yes!" I yell, throwing my hands up in the air. "I'm gay." My heart sinks, and I cup my hands over my mouth. "I hate that I told you that before I told my mom. Shit. No."

"Jesus," he says, scrunching his nose up. "Don't tell me you're gonna cry. Get out, and pull yourself together."

I gather myself, drop my hands to my hips, and lift my chin. "I'm not going anywhere until you cancel those rewrites."

He stands up, towering over me. "You need stop being so difficult and remember your place."

I don't know what comes over me, but I'm just so sick and tired of bullies. So instead of backing away, instead of recoiling like I've always done, I lean in closer and look him in the eyes.

"You need to remember where you got that episode from in the first place." My voice doesn't shake. My words don't get stuck in my throat. I don't even blink.

Malcolm, on the other hand, turns red with rage. "You better watch yourself, Becky. I can make or break you in this town. I've squashed bigger bugs than you."

"You can't fire me," I say smugly. "I'll go straight to Ms. Randall with the original script that I wrote and *you* stole."

He glares at me with a scary glint in his eyes. "You breathe one word to anyone, and I'll not only ruin you, I'll ruin Shrupty, too."

I gasp, and he smiles. "I see it now. That's why you got her the audition, right? So you could get in her pants? I respect that. She's a pretty girl; it'd be a shame to see her career destroyed."

My breathing shallows. I feel like he's ripped my heart from my chest, leaving it to bleed out on the desk between us. He's got me cornered, and he knows it. I can tell by the sick smirk on his face.

He sits down in his chair and leans back like he doesn't have a care in the world. "Now, I believe I've said everything I need to say. I'm sure you have a lot of important intern things to do. And Jane's butt cheeks must be getting cold without your lips glued to them for once." He turns the back of the chair to me. "Close the door on your way out, Becky."

I leave and pull the door closed, then stick my middle finger up against it.

"Everything okay?" Jane asks. I had no idea she was standing in the hallway.

"Oh," I say, sliding my hands into my pockets. "Yeah."

She tilts her head to the side. "You sure? You seem . . . upset."

I think about telling her what just happened. About how Malcolm took my script and turned it into trash. But I'm on thin ice already; telling Jane would only create more problems for the show and for me. Besides, what if he really does have the power to ruin Shrupty's career? I can't risk it.

"I'm fine," I say. I fake a smile, and it seems to ease her suspicions.

We start walking down the hall together, when she leans in and says, "I know he's a jackass, but there's no use arguing with him about anything. He's screwed people over many times and won."

I try to coax more detail out of her as we walk to set, but she doesn't say anything else. I think about all her interactions with Malcolm that I've witnessed, how she shrinks a little in his presence, and realize she's just as intimidated by him as I am. He must have screwed her over, too, probably more than once. All he does is treat everyone like shit. And he's going to get away with it. Again.

When we walk onto the soundstage, everything is set up to film the scene I was once so excited about but now I'm dreading. Archer stands outside the cabin door, scrolling on his phone while he waits for his cue. Shrupty sits on the couch on set, twirling her necklace between her fingers as she goes over her new lines one more time. I can still feel her kiss on my lips from when I found it on the ice on Saturday night. I still feel her hand in mine, her skin soft and tender and warm. My heart was just getting used to falling in love. Now, less than forty-eight hours later, it's all turned to shit.

The assistant director calls for everyone to get ready, and the whole set quiets down. Shrupty and Archer get into their positions, and the crew stand by for filming.

"Action!" the director calls.

Archer walks through the front door of the cabin and into the kitchen. Jane watches on the monitor, but I can't take my eyes away from Shrupty as she waits in the shadows. I can tell by the scowl on her face that she's in character, focused on playing her part even though it must be killing her more that it's killing me to watch.

The director motions for her to step onto her mark, and then Archer grabs her and pushes her against the wall. It's been rehearsed and choreographed so she doesn't get injured, but I still flinch. I hate that he's touching her like that. I hate that this is what the viewers will see instead of an epic queer love story. I hate that Shrupty has to let this homophobic douche hold a rubber knife to her throat. I'm so mad, I want to burn it all to the ground and walk away.

"Cut!" the director calls. "Okay, reset. Let's do it again."

I stand off set, quietly seething as Shrupty and Archer film the soul-crushing scene again and again for hours. Each time I hear "Action!" I die a little more inside.

CHAPTER TWENTY-FIVE

I climb up the stairs of Parker's building and drag myself to the door. My mind is spiraling into panic mode. I'm so done with today that I don't even care who sees the giant sweat stains under my armpits or down my back. There's no point trying to hide it; I'm a hot mess and everything is fucked, so being sweaty is the least of my problems. I slide the key into the door like I'm defusing a bomb, then turn it hard. But because nothing can ever be easy in my life, it doesn't work.

"Not today, Satan," I mutter, then try again. And again. And again. I grit my teeth so tight that my jaw aches, but it's better than screaming at the top of my lungs and alerting the whole neighborhood to my impending breakdown.

"Come on," I beg the door. Turn, kick, turn, shove. No matter how many times I repeat the trick Parker has shown me dozens of times, it won't fucking open. It's like it's taunting me.

"You fucking son of a bitch piece of shit." I keep muttering curses as tears fall down my cheeks. I can feel myself hanging by a thread. I crumple onto Parker's welcome mat and pull my knees up to my chest, hugging myself as I bawl my eyes out.

It wasn't supposed to be like this. Los Angeles is the City of Lights, where people come from all over the world to make their dreams come true.

What a load of shit.

The aching feeling of homesickness hits me again. I miss my mom. I miss my bed. I miss the safety of dreaming a dream that hasn't been poisoned by reality yet. The thought of leaving LA crosses my mind, and it scares me that a part of me wants to do it. A part of me wants to go home and never, ever leave Westmill again.

I'll be that old woman living alone in a dilapidated old house, sitting on the porch and talking to anyone who'll listen about the time I almost made my dreams come true.

I can't believe myself. I spent so many years trying to run away from Westmill and all my Westmill problems that I never thought about the all-new problems I'd find in LA. When I imagined my life here, I pictured palm trees and sunshine and celebrities and girls Rollerblading in bikinis. A place where I would be embraced for who I am. In Los Angeles, I could be free.

But it was all fucking lies. This town is ruled by bullies. Straight white men with all the power and connections to keep them on their thrones. This place isn't sunshine and palm trees. It's a mirage that looks like paradise from a distance, but when you get here it's just a dirty, shallow lake with a painted backdrop. Clever lighting and counterfeit smiles draw you in and then chew you up and leave you on the cutting room floor like you're nothing.

Los Angeles is where dreams come to die.

All the painful moments of the day replay in my mind. Shrupty throwing the new pages at me, the betrayal and hurt in her eyes. Having to stand by and watch while she filmed her scene with Archer, knowing there was nothing I could do. The way Malcolm treated me like I was nothing, like I didn't matter. The fact that I uttered the words *I'm gay* to him before I found the courage to say them to my own mother.

My own mother, who worked until her feet hurt and her back ached and her fingers bled to get me here. Who always made sure we had food on the table and a roof over our heads. Who never once doubted me, even when the odds were stacked against me.

That's when I pull out my phone and do something I should have done a long time ago.

I call my mom.

"Hey, baby girl!" she says when she answers, her voice filled with joy. Just hearing her call me "baby girl" makes my shoulders relax a little.

"Hey, Mama," I say.

"What's wrong?" she asks instantly.

I scoff, because what *isn't* wrong at this point? "I miss you so much." I choke back the wave of tears that threatens to spill over. "I'm so sorry I haven't called. I'm sorry I haven't replied to your texts. I'm sorry I haven't taken the time to talk to you enough since I left. I'm just . . . so sorry."

"Oh, honey," she says. "I miss you, too. The house has been so quiet without you. Your aunt Laura and I don't know what to do with ourselves."

I squeeze my eyes shut, feeling like the worst daughter in the world. "I'm so sorry."

"Thank you for saying that," she says. "I thought you'd forgotten about me." I hear her sniff back tears herself, and it breaks me. I start weeping like a child.

"No," I wail. "Never. I think about you every day. I've just been so caught up in my own shit. But it won't happen again, I swear."

"I'm not asking you to call me every day," she says, crying on the other end. "I just . . . I want to know you're okay and you're happy and safe. I want to know about LA and your writing and if you've made any new friends. I want to be part of your life."

Oh god. My chest feels like it's crumbling under the weight of heartache. "I want you to be part of my life, Mama. I want all that, too. Ugh, I'm the worst. I'm so sorry. I've been selfish, and you don't deserve it."

"Bex," she says. "I understand more than you think I do. I know being out in the world and on your own for the first time is overwhelming and scary. But it's no excuse for ignoring your family."

"You're right," I say. "It won't happen again, Mom. I promise."

"Well," she says, her tears lessening. "See that it doesn't. Now, tell me, are you okay?"

I groan into the phone. "Everything is shit today, Ma. I want to come home."

"Awww, pumpkin," she says. "Tell me everything."

And I do. Through choked-up monologues and in between gasps for air, I tell her the whole damn story—from Malcolm stealing my script, to fighting with Parker, right up to Shrupty throwing the rewrites in my face this morning.

I hear her sigh through the phone. "Baby girl. Why didn't you tell me any of this until now?"

I ponder her question for a moment, trying to find the answer. It's time to be honest with her, and with myself.

"Because I was trying to run away," I say. "I thought the only way to succeed in LA was to forget about where I'm from and reinvent myself. I was embarrassed. I'm sorry. And I'm sorry I spent so many years wanting to get away from Westmill. But most of all, I'm sorry for feeling ashamed of us. I'm sorry if I ever made you feel like we weren't good enough, or if I acted like I was better than you. I'm not better than you. I'm better *because* of you."

She's silent when I finish, and for a second I worry that our call got disconnected. "Mom?"

I hear a soft sniff and realize she's crying again.

"I'm here, baby," she says. "Thank you for saying all that."

I take in a shaky breath. "There's something else I need to say, Mama. I'm gay."

She cries harder. My heart skips a beat. Oh god. Why is she crying?

"I'm crying because I'm happy," she says, as though reading my thoughts. "I love you so *so* much, sweetie. And I'll always love you and support you, and I'll be here for you whenever you need me. But you gotta promise to call me more than once a month, you hear me?"

"Yes, Ma," I say. "I'm sorry."

"Don't apologize, do better."

"Okay, Mama."

"Now it's my turn to tell you something," she says. "There's no way in hell I'm letting you quit this and come home. I worked too hard and you worked too hard to get this far and give up now."

"But everything is so shitty right now." I wipe my nose with my knuckles, sniffing loudly.

It's like I can hear her shaking her head all the way from Washington. "Honey, sometimes life gets shitty. But you don't roll around in the shit and whine. You're not a pig. You pick yourself up, clean the shit off, and keep going."

I chuckle at her analogy. She's always had a way with words.

"This is what you're gonna do," she continues. "You're gonna pick yourself up, dust yourself off, and give 'em hell. March back into that fancy-pants studio tomorrow and unleash holy hell on that Malcolm asshole. Then find a way to make things right with that girl of yours."

"Shrupty," I say.

"Right, Shrupty," she says. "She sounds like a sweet kid, honey. Show her who you are and she'll love you, no matter where you're from."

I pause to take a breath, then ask softly, "How did you know I like her?"

She laughs. "I'm your mom. I knew the moment you said her name."

A wide, goofy smile spreads across my face. "I love you, Mom."

"Love you, too, honey. Now, go get 'em, okay?"

"Okay," I say, feeling life running through my veins again.

We end the call and I get to my feet, staring down the door again. I take in a deep breath and slide the key into the door. Turn, kick, turn, shove.

Click.

Finally, it opens.

CHAPTER TWENTY-SIX

The next day, I march back into Rosemount Studios just like my mama told me to, feeling like a new woman. I don't know how yet, but I'm determined to save queer Lyla.

I'm walking to set when a tour bus rolls past me, packed with families and tourists on vacations to Hollywood. The tour guide's voice booms through the speakers.

"Are there any *Silver Falls* fans here today?" she asks. Hands shoot up from the group. "Ah, good! We're pulling up to the *Silver Falls* stage now. I believe they're currently filming episode 612, and if you peek inside you might just catch a glimpse of some of the cast."

The bus pulls to a stop ahead, and I listen as I walk up behind it. People in the group crane their necks to see through the stage doors.

"Oh my god," a teen with dark hair and a nose ring says. I

notice they're wearing a *Silver Falls* T-shirt. "I can't believe this is the actual *SF* set! I'm dying."

Another teen snaps some photos on their phone. "Do you see anyone? Is Archer in there?"

A third teen rolls their eyes. "He's probably sucking up to Will hard-core right now, after what he said in that video."

"Seriously," the teen with the nose ring adds. "How could he say that homophobic shit when Will is supposed to be his best friend?"

The teen snapping photos frowns. "I really don't think he meant it, though. He was wasted."

"Oh," the third teen says, "he meant it. And now he's ghosting on social media, hoping people will just forget about it. Not me, though. I'm mad as hell."

They keep talking about it while the bus pulls away. If only they knew what was really going on behind those doors. They're mad now, but if they knew Malcolm had changed the whole narrative of the show to manipulate them into liking Archer again, they'd riot.

Wait a second. I stop just outside the stage, an idea forming in my mind. If the fans knew this was happening, there's no way they'd stand for it. Fandom is a powerful thing. If we all came together to protest Malcolm's straight-washing, we could save Lyla.

I look around for somewhere relatively private, then head toward the grid of trailers. Once I've found a quiet spot between an empty trailer and the outside wall of the soundstage, I take a deep breath, then make my move.

My phone shakes in my hands as I nervously open the *Silver Falls* Instagram. Notifications come pouring in, and I realize that what I'm about to do could change everything. Once I light this fire, I won't be able to control it. I could get burned. But if I don't do it, nothing will change. So I clear my throat, open up the livestream, and light the match.

"Hi, friends," I say into the camera. "I'm Bex. I'm an intern here at *Silver Falls*." I pause, suddenly having no idea what to say. The viewer count quickly rises into the thousands as I stare blankly at the screen. I let out a sigh and wipe a hand down my face.

"I don't even know where to start," I say. "But. I don't know how much time I have before someone finds me, so I'm just going to say it. You all know from the hints we've been dropping lately that a new character is joining the show. Her name is Lyla, and she's being played by Shrupty Padwal, who is the most amazing person I've ever met, and that's one of the reasons I'm so pissed about what's going on. We've also been dropping hints that Lyla is queer and has a potential romance with Sasha. At least, she *was* queer." I hear footsteps approaching and quickly duck around the corner of the trailer as they pass. I wait a moment to make sure there's no one around, then continue.

"Cut to yesterday morning," I say, a little quieter than

before. "And we all show up, ready to film Lyla's first episode. But the showrunner, Malcolm Butler, has handed out new scripts. In these new scripts, not only is Lyla straight, but she's passive, barely has any lines, and needs to be saved by Tom, who she then predictably falls for." I roll my eyes. Almost one hundred thousand people are watching the stream now. No going back.

"The moment I found out that Lyla had been straight-washed," I say, "I asked Malcolm why he did it, and he said—"

Just then, I see Dirk run past and skid to a stop when he sees me.

"Hey!" he calls. He starts storming toward me and I begin moving through the aisles of the trailer maze, trying to lose him.

I hear him shout, "I found her!" to someone and realize my time is almost up. I hurry to finish the livestream.

"He said"—I puff as I turn another corner—"it was because of the controversy surrounding Archer after his 'straight pride' speech—"

A door to one of the trailers opens in front of me, and I stop in my tracks to avoid slamming into it. Shrupty steps out of the trailer, holding her phone. My livestream is playing on her screen. When she sees me, she waves her arms at me.

"What are you doing?" she mouths at me.

I ignore her. "Malcolm rewrote Lyla into another in his long line of throwaway female characters whose sole purpose is to further the plot of the male character. And why? Because Archer felt threatened by queerness, and the showrunner is choosing to coddle him instead of actually listening to the voices of the people he hurt."

Shrupty peeks around the corner of the trailer, keeping watch while I wrap it up.

"He flipped the script and gave Archer the romance to repair the damage. Malcolm Butler erased a character's sexuality to save the reputation of a homophobe. And he thinks no one will care."

Shrupty jumps back and looks at me with panic all over her face. "Dirk!" she mouths.

"But we are Lyla," I say. "We can't let him erase us."

Just then, Shrupty snatches the phone off me and cuts the livestream off.

"Hey!" I say. "I was about to cut it."

"You're about to get cut if you don't hide," she says as she grabs me by the hand. "Come on."

She pulls me into her trailer and locks the door, then she spins around and looks at me like she's waiting for me to say something.

I shrug. "What?"

"What?" she yells, mimicking me. "That's all you're going to say? What the hell, Bex?" She keeps staring at me, her eyes wide in shock. "If this is your way of getting me to believe that you didn't do the rewrites, then fine, I believe you."

I fall back onto the couch, almost in disbelief that I actually went through with that. "I didn't know what else to do. I can't keep any more secrets." I clutch at my shirt collar and tug at it, feeling like it's choking me. "Ever since I got here I've been dodging the truth. It's tearing me up inside. And this mess with Lyla and the straight-washing is something I just can't keep quiet about."

"I totally get that," she says. "But you're going to be in so much trouble with . . ." Her phone buzzes in her hand, and her eyebrows rise.

"What?" I ask.

"*Entertainment Now* just posted an article about your livestream," she says. "It's already going viral."

"Good," I say, feeling triumphant. "Maybe all this negative press will motivate Malcolm to take back his rewrites."

"Or," Shrupty says, putting her hands on her hips, "it's going to motivate him to fire your ass."

I push my fingers through my hair and lean back against the cushions. Someone knocks on the door, and Shrupty and I freeze. She lifts her index finger to her lips, telling me to shush, then walks over to the door.

I stay quiet as she puts on a smile and opens her door. "Yes?"

I hear Dirk's voice. "Have you seen that intern?"

Shrupty tilts her head to the side. "Hmm, you're going to have to be more specific?"

Dirk groans. I try to stamp out the panic rising in my chest.

"The intern," he says. "Red hair, glasses, talks too much. You're with her all the time."

Talks too much? Screw this guy. I stand up, ready to talk his ear right off, but Shrupty holds a hand up to me behind the door.

"Haven't seen anyone fitting that description," Shrupty says before swinging the door closed and locking it again.

We wait for him to walk away, then Shrupty comes toward me and puts her hands on my shoulders.

"You need to chill," she says. "You have this super-wild look in your eyes that's freaking me out."

"Sorry," I say as I force myself back down on the couch. She's right; I'm wound way too tight right now. I close my eyes and take in a slow, deep breath. "Do you ever have one of those days where you just feel like everything you've ever believed was a lie and everything you've ever dreamed about was built directly on top of those lies?"

Shrupty scoffs. "About once a week, yeah."

"Okay. Phew." I laugh sarcastically. "As long as it's not just me."

Shrupty sits next to me, her hair falling to one side. "Can I ask you something?"

I nod, and she drops her gaze to the floor. "What did you mean before when you said you've been dodging the truth?"

My stomach turns from nerves, but I'm done hiding parts of who I am from people I care about.

"I didn't go to prom."

She looks at me, her eyes narrowed. "Huh?"

I shift on the couch so I'm facing her. "At Will's party, I told you I went to prom. But I didn't. I worked the night shift at Sonic, where I worked every night. You won prom king. Well, the king and queen of my prom banned me from going because I wasn't cool enough, then they showed up at Sonic after and threw fries at me. And even if I wanted to go, I had no money for a suit because I was saving up to come to LA for this internship."

"Oh my god," she says. "They threw fries at you?"

I nod. "You said your high school days were the best days. It wasn't like that for me. Not by a long shot. High school was a nightmare. Those weren't the best days of my life . . . *these are.* These days spent in the writers' room and on set and with you . . . I've never been happier in my entire life. I'm doing work I love, I've made friends, I met you." I pause, suddenly hit by the weight of what I've done. "And I'm probably about to lose all of it."

Shrupty reaches out and takes my hand. "Not all of it. It doesn't matter to me how rich you are or how popular you were in high school. Money isn't that important."

I let out a bitter laugh. "See, you say that, but it is. Money matters a lot, especially when you don't have it. People love to talk about poverty like it's romantic or grounding or"—I roll my eyes—"character building. But it's stressful. It's traumatic. It's, like, ninety percent of why I'm so anxious all the time. It's the reason my mom is going to be working until she's dead. Unless I can find a good job and earn enough to help her out." I choke back tears.

Shrupty gently rubs my back, and her touch is the only thing holding me together. "Why didn't you tell me any of this?"

I take my glasses off and wipe my eyes on the back of my hand. "I was embarrassed. I was ashamed of who I am and where I come from, but I'm not anymore. I worked my ass off to get to LA, and my mom worked her ass off her whole life to give me more opportunities than she ever had. That's nothing to be ashamed of. I see that now."

"See," Shrupty says quietly. "That's something I can relate to. My parents worked their asses off, too. They were immigrants who left their home and their families to come here and give me and my brother a different life. They're wealthy now, but it wasn't always that way for them. My mom studied for years in Mumbai and here in LA to get where she is now. And my dad worked three jobs while she was pregnant with me and getting ready to graduate. Even though my family is wealthy now, my parents have always hustled for it. Just like your mom hustles for you. You definitely shouldn't be ashamed of that. You should be proud."

My heart swells. Hearing her open up to me like that means the world. She's trusting me with her story, just like I'm trusting her with mine.

"Thank you for telling me all that." I notice the rewritten scenes on her coffee table, and I look Shrupty in her eyes. "I swear, I had nothing to do with the rewrites. It was all Malcolm."

She pushes a loose strand of hair behind my ear, sending a shiver down my spine.

"You probably just nuked your internship to stop the rewrites," she says. "So I believe you. But why did he put your name on the script?"

"Because I wrote the original version," I say. "And he stole it. I confronted him about it, and we reached a compromise: I would get a writing credit on the final script. I would never have agreed to that if I'd known he was going to do this."

Shrupty stands up and starts pacing back and forth. "This fucking guy." She squeezes her hands into fists. "He can't get away with this. He's everything I hate about this fucking town. We need to do something."

I stand up and walk over to her. "Okay, I know you're pissed. So am I. But don't do anything reckless. I already screwed myself with that livestream, and we won't fix anything if we both get ourselves fired."

She pulls me into a hug. "Now that I know everything, I honestly don't blame you for doing that livestream. People need to know what's going on. None of this is okay, and Malcolm needed to be called out."

"So," I say, resting my cheek on her shoulder. "Does this mean you're not mad at me? We're good?"

Shrupty leans back to look me in the eyes. "We're good." Then she gives me a soft, sweet kiss that makes me weak at the knees. Her hands thread through my hair while mine follow the curves of her hips.

A knock on the door interrupts our tender moment.

"Yes?" Shrupty calls, then moves her kisses down my neck, sending little electric shocks on my skin.

"We need you on set in five!" a voice calls from outside.

Shrupty groans, and calls back, "On my way!" She kisses me again before stepping back. "Sorry, I have to go film more scenes with Archer." She makes a face when she says his name, and I feel awful for her.

She picks up her phone and the script, then turns to me. "You need to stay here. Don't leave and don't let anyone in. They can't fire you if they can't find you."

"Okay," I say. "Good plan. I'll just live here forever."

She laughs dryly. "I'll be back later and we'll figure out what to do next, okay?"

I nod, and she kisses me one more time before she leaves.

CHAPTER TWENTY-SEVEN

I must've fallen asleep. I'm on the couch in Shrupty's trailer, woken by the sound of my phone ringing. I can tell it's Gabby because I set it to play the *Silver Falls* theme when she calls.

"Hey," I say, my voice croaky from sleeping.

"I can't believe my best friend is internet famous" is the first thing she says. "I stan a legend."

I laugh as I sit up and stretch my back. "You saw my livestream?"

"I missed it," she says. "But I've seen the fallout. *Silver Falls* is trending, and the first thing I saw when I clicked on it was your face! And man, you looked mad as hell."

"I was," I say. "I am."

"Well," she says. "I signed the petition and shared it. I want to help, so if there's anything you need—"

"Wait." I reach over to open Shrupty's laptop on the coffee table. "What petition?"

"Some people from the fandom launched a petition hours ago," she says. "It's already got over ten thousand signatures."

"Seriously?" I open Google and type "Silver Falls" into the search bar. Instantly, dozens of headlines pop up about my livestream. "Whoa. *HuffPost Queer Voices* picked it up? And *Out* magazine! Jesus, *Teen Vogue*, too!"

"Mhmm," Gabby says. "I'm telling you, you're a viral star. A call-out queen!"

I put Gabs on speaker and place the phone in my lap, then log in to my Twitter. "I have over a thousand follow requests."

I hear Gabby gasp. "May as well go public now. Give the people what they want, Bex."

I giggle nervously and switch my profile to public. My mentions are filled with support from *Silver Falls* fans and interview requests from media outlets.

"Well," I say with a sigh. "I'm definitely getting fired over this."

Gabby laughs like I said something hilarious. "No way, dude. Have you seen the backlash that Malcolm guy is getting right now? If he fires you for speaking out against erasing a gay character, people will riot online."

She makes an interesting point. "You think?"

"Bex," she says, her voice suddenly serious. "You have the

whole fandom behind you. Including me. I just wish I was there so I could riot with you."

"I wish you were here, too," I say. "How are you, anyway?"

She sighs into the phone. "Bored. Sleeping in was fun at first, but literally all I do is hang at home and watch TV with my mom. Even the dog is sick of me. This town is no fun without you."

"Just come to LA," I say, half jokingly. "I miss my best friend."

"If I had the money for a bus ticket," she says, "I'd be there in a second."

"I know."

There's a pause in the conversation, and I take it as my chance to finally come out to her. I swallow my nerves and take the phone off speaker.

"So, um," I start, squeezing my eyes shut. "I want to tell you something."

"Yeah?" she says, curiosity in her voice.

"I'm very gay."

I say it so smoothly this time that I surprise myself. Don't get me wrong, it's still not easy. Coming out takes guts and energy, and I low-key resent the fact that it's something I even have to do.

"Wow," Gabby says. "Okay. Cool."

I tap my feet anxiously on the floor. "Cool?"

"Yeah," she says. I swear I can hear a smile in her voice.

"Cool. I mean, not gonna lie, it's not like a huge shock or anything." She giggles, and so do I. "I'm happy for you, Bex, and I'm glad you told me. Dammit, now I really wish I was there so I could give you a giant hug."

I sit on the phone with her for a few more minutes, just talking and laughing about nothing much in particular. When we say good-bye, I stretch out on the couch, unable to wipe the happy smile from my face.

. . .

By the time 5:00 P.M. rolls around, I'm deep into the passionate Twitter discussions about Lyla's straight-washing. The fandom has exploded into action all over the world in an effort to save Lyla and Sasha's romance—even coming up with a ship name: Lasha. #SaveLasha is trending number two on Twitter, followed by #DontHideYourGays. #WeAreLyla is number one. Queer celebrities and activists are posting the petition and sharing their own stories of times they, too, were pressured to hide or were erased completely by the Hollywood powers that be. My video has made it onto *BuzzFeed*, *Variety*, and NBC.

Meanwhile, Malcolm, Archer, and the network have been strangely silent. No one has issued a statement or tried to defend themselves in any way. It makes me nervous about what they're planning.

Just as I'm reading a long Twitter thread dissecting the ways erasing Lyla's queerness intersects with race and gender, Shrupty returns from filming. And she's carrying takeout.

"Thank god you're still here," she says as she drops the bags on the counter in the kitchenette. "I was worried you'd left. People have been asking me where you are. The whole studio is on damage control."

I walk over to help unpack the food. It smells so good that it makes my stomach rumble. "I'm so hungry."

"I figured you would be," she says. "I ordered Chinese food on Postmates."

"Yum," I say. We carry the food over to the couch and start eating. "How did your scenes go?"

She cringes. "Archer was even more unbearable than usual. He's obsessing about what you said in the livestream. In between takes he was all, 'I never asked for these rewrites' and 'It wasn't fair of her to throw me under the bus like that.'" She rolls her eyes. "Like he's the victim in all this."

I swallow my rice and wipe my mouth with one of the paper napkins. "Ugh. I'm so sorry you had to hear that all night."

She shrugs. "It's okay. The more he whined, the less acting I had to do in our fight scenes. I must've thrown him against the wall twenty times today. Sure, he had wires doing most of the work for me, but still. It felt good to overpower him, even if it was pretend."

While we eat, I update her on what's happening online.

Her beautiful brown eyes watch me eagerly as I list all the articles, hashtags, and celebrities talking about her character.

"Holy shit," she says once I've told her everything. "You broke the internet. I gotta see this." She sits on the floor between the couch and the coffee table and opens her laptop, finding the petition first. "Almost fifteen thousand signatures!"

She turns to me, a wide smile on her face. "All of this? It could save Lyla."

"You really think so?"

Shrupty nods, then opens up a blank Word doc on her laptop. "There's just one more thing this rebellion needs."

She starts typing, and the words on the screen make me smile.

Statement from Shrupty Padwal regarding #DontHideYourGays.

. . .

An hour later, I'm sitting on the couch behind Shrupty, braiding her hair while she reads over her statement one more time.

"Okay," she says. "How does this sound? 'On Monday morning, I was excited to begin filming my first guest starring role on *Silver Falls*. I was ecstatic to be a queer brown girl playing a queer brown girl on a show that—aside from the incredible Alyssa Huntington—has been canonically white, cishet, and male. But when I arrived, I discovered not only had the episode been rewritten, but so had my character. Today, I discovered the reasoning behind those changes—to protect the more famous, more powerful straight white male lead. A male lead who, just a couple of days ago, I personally heard give a drunken, disgruntled speech about the queer community.'"

I fist pump the air while she keeps reading aloud.

"'But am I surprised? No. I'm not surprised, because this happens all too often. And it will continue to happen unless we speak up. People in power are counting on our silence, but I will not go quietly. I know I'm going to catch a lot of heat for this. I'll be labeled a "difficult woman" for speaking my mind. But I am prepared for that. It's more important to me that people know this is happening, that it's not okay. So keep raising your voices. I truly believe we can save Lyla and make sure people in power here in Hollywood never do this again.'"

I lean forward and kiss her on her cheek. "You are such a badass."

She blushes and turns so she can kiss me. "Back at you, girl."

"You ready for this?" I ask.

Shrupty raises an eyebrow at me. "I was born ready. Let's light this match."

At 9:00 P.M., Shrupty posts her statement on all her social media channels. Then, we lie on the couch together and watch the fire spread online until long past midnight.

CHAPTER TWENTY-EIGHT

When I wake up the next morning, Shrupty is in the shower and I have an e-mail from Dirk on my phone.

Bex,
Malcolm would like to meet with you to discuss the rewrites.
Please be at his office at 9am.
Dirk

I read over it again, looking for signs of how much trouble I'm in. He called me Bex and not just "intern," so that's promising. And he said Malcolm wants to talk about the rewrites. Hope rises in my chest. Could we have saved Lyla?

I shoot Shrupty a quick text to let her know where I'm going, then step out of the trailer. It's eight forty-five, so I need to go straight to the production building, but I stop when I see Archer sitting on the steps of his trailer. He's on the phone with someone, and he looks stressed as he clutches his hair in his hand.

"Will," he says into the phone. "This isn't my fault. I didn't ask him to write her straight."

I try to sneak past him, but he sees me.

"I'll call you back," he says before ending the call and looking up at me. "I never meant for any of this to happen."

I let out a sigh. "Whether you meant it or not, it happened. I gotta go."

"Wait," he calls after me, reaching out a hand. "I want to fix it. Please, tell me what I should do."

I narrow my eyes at him. "Dude, I'm not your queer Yoda. Anyway, I'm sure your PR team is working overtime to spin this in a way that benefits you. Malcolm sure is."

He waves a hand dismissively. "It's not that I'm worried about. I want to make things right with Will. And Alyssa, Shrupty, you. Everyone I hurt."

I have to admit, I'm surprised. I turn to look at him, searching his eyes to see if he's telling the truth.

"For real," he says. "I fucked up. Will is like a brother to me. I feel like the worst person ever for hurting him and ruining his party." He drops his head in his hands. Part of me wants to leave him here to sort out his own shit, but for some reason I just can't walk away. So, with a sigh, I sit down next to him.

"Why did you say all that at the party, man?" I ask, annoyance clear in my tone. "And don't say it was just because you were drunk, because I will kick you to the curb so fast."

He shakes his head. "I keep asking myself the same question. I didn't mean any of it. But I'm not gonna try and make excuses. I had a bad night, and I lashed out. I took it out on my friends. I regretted it the moment it happened."

"Well," I say, resting my elbows on my knees. "Your job is to unpack the reasons behind why you did what you did. Educate yourself on why what you said was hurtful to the queer community, and while you're at it, educate yourself on issues facing black folks, people of color, indigenous communities, disabled people, because they all intersect with each other. Follow leaders in the social justice movement—and fucking listen to them." I clench my hands into fists and slam them against my knees. "You have such a huge freakin' platform, man. Do you know how much good you could do with that if you ever thought about people other than yourself?"

I feel myself getting riled up, so I pause to take a calming breath. "Anyway, before this turns into a TED Talk, I just have one more thing to say: Apologize to Will. And Shrupty, Alyssa, everyone. Release a statement that isn't a fake-ass non-apology. No more 'I'm sorry, buts.' A real apology that doesn't make excuses. I'm not saying it will make everything chill again, because it probably won't. But it's a start. Everyone fucks up, but few people are willing to swallow their pride enough to actually apologize and try to do better."

When I stop, he's staring at me like I just told a joke he doesn't get. "That seems excessive, don't you think? I mean, I'm happy to apologize again, but all that other stuff sounds like a ton of work."

Oh, right. He doesn't *actually* care. My blood boils like acid in my veins. I immediately stand up and start walking away.

"Hey!" he calls after me. "Where are you going?"

I wave a hand behind me, dismissing him and his bullshit. "I've wasted enough of my time on you."

. . .

When I walk into Malcolm's office at 9:00 A.M., he's sitting at his desk with a man I've never seen before. The stranger adjusts his tie and stands up, gesturing for me to sit down.

"Miss Phillips," he says with a nod. "Welcome. I'm Mr. Butler's attorney."

My heart freezes, cracks down the middle, and shatters into a thousand pieces. I am so dead.

The attorney slides a piece of paper over to me and hands me a pen. I'm so numb from fear that I take it.

"This," he says, "is what we call a nondisclosure agreement. You need to sign it."

I scan the paper, but I'm too freaked out to process anything coherently. Words like *legally binding, irreparable injury,* and *money damages* jump out at me, scaring me to my core. I see my name, Shrupty's name, and Malcolm's name. But the document is five pages long and filled with legal terminology that I can't even begin to understand, even if I wasn't in panic mode.

"Wh-what is this for?" I ask, my voice trembling.

The attorney leans forward, his gaze searing into me. "This is to confirm that you will refrain from discussing or revealing to anyone that my client, Mr. Butler, ever misused or discredited your original work, either intentionally or otherwise."

"Why is Shrupty mentioned here?" I ask, pointing to her name on the second page.

"As it says right there in black and white," the attorney continues, "if you agree to these terms, Mr. Butler will rewrite the role of Lyla to the original sexual orientation for a total of one episode, and one episode only, to be played by Shrupty Padwal."

I nod slowly, trying to wrap my mind around their proposal. A sick feeling in my stomach tells me I shouldn't sign anything they give me, and that one episode with a queer Lyla is not enough.

"I don't know," I say.

The attorney shakes his head. "I hope you understand the gravity of this situation. Mr. Butler is being incredibly generous with this offer, and because of that it expires the moment you leave this room."

Then, he leans in to whisper something in Malcolm's ear. Malcolm groans but nods, and the lawyer turns back to me.

"To sweeten this offer," he says, "Malcolm has agreed to pay you the fifteen thousand dollars you are owed for cowriting this episode."

My jaw drops. "Did you say fifteen thousand dollars?"

The lawyer nods and gives Malcolm a sideways glance. "It should have been offered to you once the script was approved. But it seems Mr. Butler forgot to mention it to you."

Yeah, I bet he forgot. I want to cry, to call my mom, to fade into nothing. I can't believe what I'm hearing. He's offering me almost as much money as my mom makes in a year. All I have to do is sign this form.

"What if I don't sign it?" I ask.

Malcolm and his lawyer exchange a look, then the attorney turns back to me. "If you refuse to comply, my client will have no choice but to remove you from the internship program and replace you with someone more deserving of the role. There are plenty of promising young talents who would do anything for the opportunity you've been so generously given. And of course, you wouldn't get one cent of the fifteen thousand dollars."

I clutch the pen in my clammy hand, holding it over the last page of the NDA. If I sign it, we get queer Lyla, even just for an episode. Shrupty gets to launch her acting career with a groundbreaking role. And I'll get to keep my internship and have all my financial worries wiped clean.

I look over the pages one more time and catch something I missed earlier. "'Defend the client and studio in a statement release'? What does that mean?"

The attorney's gaze falls to the table. "You will release a statement to the media, backing up Mr. Butler's upcoming statement, declaring that your livestream and Shrupty Padwal's statement were a complete fabrication. You will also defend Mr. Butler and Mr. Archer Carlton against the ridiculous accusations of homophobia."

My jaw drops. "You want me to say it was all a hoax? To call Shrupty a liar and defend Archer's hurtful words?"

"If you want to keep your position," he adds, his voice low, "you will comply."

I put the pen down on the table. "You have no right to ask me to do this."

He smiles, but it's unfriendly, like how a Disney villain smiles right before he pushes the hero off a cliff. "I assure you, Miss Phillips, we are well within our rights. And let me remind you that Mr. Butler could have easily fired you without giving you this chance to stay on as an intern. This is your best and only option."

They're trying to intimidate me, and it's working. But I'd rather spend the rest of my life taking orders from my old high school bullies at Westmill Sonic than stay in LA knowing I threw Shrupty under the bus and sold my soul. Malcolm knows I can't afford a lawyer. He knows I need this internship to turn into a career. He knows how desperate I am to write for television. He's trying to exploit all that to save his own ass.

"So," the attorney says. "Sign the agreement and we can all move on."

"No," I say. "I'm not signing anything."

Malcolm finally speaks. "Sign it, or you're fired."

I shrug my shoulders. "So fire me."

He picks up the receiver on his desk and calls for security. My fear has been replaced with righteousness and adrenaline. We sit in determined, angry silence until two men come to get me. They wait while I collect my things from the writers' room, mostly my water bottle and some notebooks.

Jane walks in just as I'm leaving, her eyes widening when she sees my entourage of two security guards.

"Are you okay?" she asks me.

"Not really," I say. "But I'm glad you're here. I want to thank you for taking me under your wing. You're an amazing writer, and I'm so glad I got to work with you. Good luck."

The guards usher me down the hall, and Jane watches in shock. Malcolm stands in the doorway of his office, smirking at me as I walk past. I ignore him, holding my head up high even though all I want to do is fall to the floor and cry. But I'd never let him see how upset he's made me. I wouldn't give him the satisfaction of knowing he's hurt me.

I try to keep my composure as I leave the building, the

guards walking on either side of me. People walking by stop and stare. I spot Dirk up ahead, carrying a takeout bag from the bakery Malcolm likes. An evil grin spreads across his face when he sees me.

"Bye, Felicia!" he calls as I walk by. I flip both my middle fingers at him.

Suddenly, I hear footsteps running up behind me, and for a frightening second I think Dirk is coming for me, but when I look over my shoulder I see Shrupty chasing after us.

"Hey!" she yells. "What's going on?"

"Malcolm fired me," I tell her. I try to stop walking so I can talk to her, but one of the guards ushers me on.

Shrupty runs ahead of us, holding her arms out to try to stop us. "No. Just wait. He can't do this." She looks tiny standing in front of these two big, burly men, but the fire in her eyes is enough to make anyone think twice about crossing her.

"It's already been done," one of them says. "Keep it moving."

Shrupty starts walking backward and pulls her phone out of her back pocket. "Fine. If that's how they wanna play, then let's play." A crowd starts to gather as she records the scene on her phone. "If Bex is fired for doing a livestream and speaking out, then I guess I'm fired, too."

I shake my head at her. "Shrupty—"

"What?" she asks, keeping her camera trained on me. "If Malcolm wants you out, then I'm out, too."

"No," I say. "Don't—"

But she stops me again. "Are you trying to tell me what to do?"

That's when I shut up. No way am I going against her when she's on fire like this. I raise my palms to show her I give in, and she nods.

"That's what I thought," she says. Then she takes my hand. "Come on. We're leaving."

Shrupty holds her phone up so the people watching her livestream can see the guards following us into the parking lot. Once we're in her car, she speaks into the camera.

"This isn't the end," she says, her voice filled with determination. "He thinks he's won, but he can't finish this episode without me, and I won't set foot back on set until the Lyla we were all promised returns and Bex gets her internship back."

One of the guards knocks on her driver's-side window and gestures for us to move on.

"Okay," Shrupty says, exasperated. "We're leaving. We're leaving!"

She ends the livestream and starts her car, backing out of the parking spot so fast that her tires squeal. I can't help but just stare at her as she grits her teeth and clutches the steering wheel. I've never been more attracted. The energy coming off her is electric, and the way she stood up for me like that in front of everyone . . . My chest swells with emotion as we drive out of the studio lot and onto the road. She glances at me out of the corner of her eye, but I still can't look away.

"What?" she asks, suddenly appearing self-conscious.

I smile a little. "No one has ever done anything like that for me before."

"Oh," she says with a shrug, like it's no big deal. "Well, I wasn't going to just stand by while my girlfriend gets fired like that."

My heart flutters in my chest. "What did you just say?"

She furrows her brow. "Which part?"

A smile grows on my face, and I couldn't wipe it away even if I wanted to. "The part where you called me your girlfriend."

Shrupty gives me a sideways glance and scratches her head. "I did?"

I keep grinning. "Yep."

"Well," she stutters. "I mean. Yeah. Unless you want me to call you something else?"

I reach over and take her hand. "No way. I love it." I giggle, and she squeezes my hand. "Girlfriend."

She smiles back at me, her features softening. "So, girlfriend, what do we do now?"

"I have absolutely no idea." I rest my head back on the seat, replaying the morning over in my mind. "But we can't give up on Lyla."

"Never," she says. "We have to keep this fire lit. We're like

Thelma and Louise, fighting the system together. Except without cowboy Brad Pitt or the whole cliff-dive at the end."

We drive around for a while, listening to one of Shrupty's playlists, titled "Big Dick Energy," and doing our best "Carpool Karaoke" impressions. Nothing pumps you up after being fired like screaming Demi's "Sorry Not Sorry" at the top of your lungs.

. . .

Later, we're sitting at a table at Shrupty's aunt's restaurant, sharing a piece of rainbow-colored cake and trying to figure out our next move.

"This isn't the end, right?" Shrupty asks, her brow wrinkled in worry. "We still have the whole fandom behind us. We can't let them down."

"No," I agree. "This isn't the end. It's more like a cliff-hanger. Or a plot twist."

She raises an eyebrow. "I like that. Okay, you're the writer here, so tell me. If this was an episode, what would happen next?"

"Getting fired and making a huge scene about it would definitely make for good TV," I say, chuckling. Then I sit back in my chair, considering her words. "When I'm plotting an episode, there's always a moment when everything that could go wrong does go wrong. I call it the SHTF moment: the Shit Hits the Fan moment."

Shrupty laughs. "So that's the part of the episode we're in right now. Shit has hit the fan."

"Definitely," I say, nodding. "We're Bella, writhing in pain on the floor of the ballet studio in *Twilight*. Or Princess Anna, betrayed by Hans and locked in a freezing-cold room in *Frozen*."

"Or Thor," she says, "overpowered by Hela in *Ragnarok*."

"Yes! We just need to find our biggest lightning blast in the history of lightning."

The waiter comes over with our drinks, and the moment I get my coffee, I dump a spoonful of sugar into it.

"Mostly," I say with a sigh as I watch the sugar dissolve into the coffee and stir it with my spoon, "I just want the fandom to see how amazing Sasha and Lyla are together."

Shrupty takes a sip of her bloodred strawberry shake. "Okay, so let's do that."

"How?" I ask. "It's not like we can film the episode ourselves."

"Why not?" she asks. I furrow my brow, wondering if she's joking.

I start listing on my fingers. "We don't have any camera equipment, or actors, or permission, or money."

"Um, hello?" Mimicking me, Shrupty counts on her fingers,

too. "I have camera equipment, I'm literally Lyla, we can use your original script so we don't need permission, and if we already have cameras, talent, and a story, we don't need that much money."

I give her a look that says "give me a break," and she chuckles. "Okay, so it won't be worthy of an Emmy or anything, but who cares? It's the message that matters."

"True," I say, nodding. "We could pick the best Lasha scene and film that. Or make a mock trailer for the episode."

"Yes!" Shrupty gets out her phone and starts typing. "We just need one more person on board if we want to do this right." She lifts her phone to her ear and a moment later perks up. "Hey, Alyssa?"

While she asks Alyssa to join our rogue mission, I text Gabby. This is too big for me to do it without my ride-or-die, and I'm determined to get her to LA. Using some of my savings to buy her a bus ticket will be worth it just to see her face.

Bex: hey

Gabby: hey!

Bex: you wanna join a rebellion?

Gabby: always.

CHAPTER TWENTY-NINE

The next day, Parker and I pull up to the bus station, and I'm so excited I could burst.

"There she is!" I say, pointing to Gabby as she walks out the sliding doors of the station, carrying a duffel bag. I jump out of the car and run to her, arms spread wide.

"Bex!" she calls when she sees me. She drops her bag and I leap into her arms, cuddling her close.

"I can't believe you're actually here," I say. Happy tears spill over my cheeks.

Gabby squeals. "Thank you so much for buying my ticket."

Parker toots his horn. "Get in, losers! We've got a rebellion to launch!"

Gabby pumps her fists in the air. "Let's go!"

I pick up her bag and we walk hand in hand to the car, giggling like we did when we were little.

Not long after, Parker pulls up to Shrupty's front gate and

leans out the window to press the button. Gabby's jaw drops as the gates open and we roll down the driveway.

"Whoa," she says. "I feel like a Kardashian right now."

We walk up the steps and Shrupty opens the door before I even ring the bell. She jumps into my arms, squeezing me tight.

"You ready for this?" she asks as she lets go.

"You bet." I turn to Gabby, grinning from ear to ear. "Gabby, this is my girlfriend, Shrupty. Shrupty, this Gabby, my best friend."

They hug each other, then Shrupty hugs Parker before inviting us inside.

After we all take off our shoes, she grabs my hand and leads us through the house and down into the basement.

Alyssa is waiting on the couch in front of the big-screen TV, and I'm surprised to see Will sitting next to her.

"I told Will about your plan," Alyssa says when we sit with them. "And he wanted in."

Will nods, his brow pinched in concern. "I want to help save Lyla."

"Thank you," I say to them. "Really. Having you both stand by us on this will strengthen our message a lot."

"Okay," Shrupty says as she stands up. "This is the plan: We're going to film it like an episode trailer. That way, we won't spoil too much of the story line, but we still get to show the world how much potential the Lasha arc has. Then we're going to post it to my YouTube channel. Cool?" Everyone nods. "Okay! Operation Make It Gay is a go!"

. . .

An hour later, we're all set up in Shrupty's basement, preparing to start shooting. Gabby and Will help Shrupty set up her camera, lighting equipment, and green screen—all perks of being a professional YouTuber. Alyssa is sitting on the couch while Parker does her makeup, and I'm pacing back and forth nervously. I'm reading over the script for the millionth time, making sure I've picked out the best lines and scenes to showcase in the trailer.

Our goal is to have the video ready to upload on Friday morning, so we have a ton of work to do and not much time to do it. But I'm not worried—I have the best damn team in the world.

Gabby skips over to me, and I can feel her excitement buzzing off her.

"I can't believe I'm hanging out with these people!" she whispers. "Will Horowitz! Alyssa Huntington! Shrupty Padwal! How do you do this every day and not freak the fuck out?"

I glance over at my new squad, my heart overflowing with gratitude. "It's easy when they're all such great, down-to-earth people." Then I take Gabby by the shoulders and look her in the eye. "I'm so happy you're here. You're the best ride-or-die a girl could ever ask for. I love you, Gabs."

She blushes, then pulls me in for a hug. "I love you, too, Bex. You've never said that to me before."

I nod against her shoulder. "I know. I'm trying to be better at telling people how I feel and letting them in."

Gabby lets out a happy sigh. "I'm so proud of you. I've never seen you more . . . *yourself.*"

"Stop," I say, clearing my throat. "You're gonna make me cry."

"Aaaand she's back," Gabby says with a chuckle.

"I'm a work in progress." I let go of her, and she nods knowingly.

"Aren't we all?" Then she gives me a playful slap on the arm. "Now go make some quality gay content."

CHAPTER THIRTY

"Okay," I say as I stand behind the camera. Shrupty, Will, and Alyssa are on their marks. On a real set, gaffer tape would be used to show them where to stand, but Shrupty's mom was not about to let us get tape stuck to her carpet, so we improvised and used yellow Post-it notes. "This is where Lyla catches up to Sasha and Will and tells them she wants to help them fight her family."

Alyssa and Will nod. Shrupty shakes out her arms and legs to loosen herself up. She looks worried.

"Shrupty," I say. "You okay?"

She nods but then turns to Alyssa and Will. "I just want to make sure you're both one hundred percent cool to go through with this. We could all be risking a lot. So if you have any doubts, now's the time to back out. We won't blame you."

"I'm in," Alyssa says.

Will nods. "One hundred percent."

"We're both so done with Malcolm and his bullshit," Alyssa adds. "This was the last straw."

"And I can't keep making excuses for Archer," Will says. "All I've done since season one is try to convince myself that he's my friend. But that rant at my party the other night? That wasn't the first time I've heard him say stuff like that. I'm not going to let it slide anymore."

Alyssa puts her arm around him, and he gives her a sad smile.

Just then, the door to the basement opens and we hear footsteps coming down the stairs. We all turn to see who it is. Shrupty's dad stops halfway down when he sees all of us standing there, surrounded by cameras and bright lights and a green screen propped against the wall.

"Um," he says, almost like he's shy. "Hello, strangers in my basement."

"Dad," Shrupty sighs. "This is a closed set."

He narrows his eyes, glancing at each of us. "Your mother wanted me to ask if your friends are staying for dinner."

"We're just gonna order pizza or something," Shrupty says. "Got a long night of filming ahead of us."

"What . . . what's happening here?" he asks.

Shrupty giggles at her dad's confused expression. "Oh, nothing. We're just rebelling against the heteronormative culture that permeates our current media climate."

Her dad stares at us blankly for a second, then shrugs. "Okeydokey. Keep up the good work." And with that, he turns around and goes back up the stairs. "Honey," he calls to his wife. "Did you know there's a rebellion happening in our basement?" Then the door clicks closed, and we all burst into laughter.

With the mood lightened and everyone in their places, we're ready to film.

"Okay?" I ask. "Action!" I can't wipe the grin off my face. I feel so cool for calling out "action," like a real director.

. . .

The dirt and gravel crunch under our sneakers as we follow the hiking trail up the mountain. We purposely chose the hardest, rockiest trail because it's the least populated, and we need as much privacy as possible to get this scene done tonight. We don't exactly have any of the permits you're supposed to get when filming in public spaces. That's also why we've packed all our equipment and props in picnic baskets, coolers, and backpacks—to any onlookers, we're just a group of friends heading out for a picnic and stargazing above LA.

Parker has a styling gig tonight, and Will had to go back to Rosemount to keep shooting the "official" version of episode 612, so it's just me, Shrupty, Alyssa, and Gabby for the night shoot.

"Remember," Shrupty says as she adjusts the strap of her backpack. "We need to start hiking back down at nine thirty. Security guards start their checks at ten."

"Got it," Alyssa says. She's leading the way, having hiked this trail a few times before. Shrupty is behind her, followed by me, and then Gabby, who is living for the view of Los Angeles below.

"I can't believe I'm in Hollywood," she says excitedly. I grin at her over my shoulder and reach back to squeeze her hand.

"I'm so happy you're here," I say. I gaze out at the view beneath us, the multimillion-dollar homes nestled into the Los Feliz mountainside, the buildings reaching up to the sky from downtown LA, their glass exteriors sparkling in the sun as it begins its descent over the horizon. This is what I dreamed about from my bed in Westmill.

My foot catches on a branch, but I steady myself before I fall. From then on, I keep my gaze off the view and on the trail. The basket I'm holding has all Shrupty's camera equipment in it; the last thing I want to do is break it with my clumsiness.

We're heading to Cedar Grove, a wooded section of Griffith Park that Alyssa says resembles the outdoor cabin set on *Silver Falls*. The higher up the mountain we go, the more lush and dense the forest becomes. Tonight, we're filming the opening scene of the episode: Sasha running through the woods and getting trapped by a hunter's net, only to be released by Lyla.

"I love this city," Shrupty says as she takes in a deep breath of the fresh air. She looks adorable today, in a short olive-green romper, matching bandanna tied around her head, and her hair up in a messy bun.

"You look like a sexy Rambo," I whisper in her ear from behind. She bites her bottom lip, then laughs.

"This is my very professional director's outfit," she explains, pausing to pose on the trail. "I wanted to look cute for my short film directorial debut."

"Ava DuVernay would be proud," I say.

Soon, we reach Cedar Grove and unload all our stuff in a small clearing with a picnic table. The pink sky stretches out past the trees, and the city lights grow brighter by the second.

"What do you think?" Alyssa asks as she stands in the middle of the clearing. "Is it Silver Falls–y enough?"

Shrupty inspects the area. "If we shoot it just right, we can make it work." She lifts her tripod out of one of the baskets. "It's all about the angles."

I know I should be as focused on the project as she is, but I just can't take my eyes off her. I smile to myself in a way that I never did before I met Shrupty.

Gabby pokes me in the ribs to get my attention. "You're so cute."

I pretend I wasn't just checking out my girlfriend—oh, how I love calling her that. "Huh?"

"The way you look at her . . . ," she says quietly so only I can hear her. "I've never seen you look at anyone like that. It's like when you're a kid and you see a rainbow and have to stop to just admire it."

My cheeks warm. "Is it that obvious?"

Gabby grins. "She's your rainbow."

My heart grows ten times its size.

"Shut up," I say with a giggle, my cheeks flushed in embarrassment. Gabby rolls her eyes at me.

"Just own it," she says, throwing an arm around me. "I see what's happening here, and I'm living for it. Love looks good on you."

Tingles run down the back of my neck, and I drop my gaze. "Thanks, Gabs. She is my rainbow."

Alyssa opens one of the backpacks and gasps. "Whoa." She lifts the wolf mask out of the bag and inspects it closely. "This is creepy. I love it." We don't exactly have the budget or the special effects skills to CGI a werewolf, so a mask and tons of close-ups will have to do.

Shrupty walks over and touches one of the ears, then squirms. "God, it's so real." She turns to me. "Remind me later to give Parker a big thank-you hug."

Parker pulled some strings and managed to score the eerily realistic wolf mask from a prop house. "We have to be very careful with it," I say. "It's on loan and needs to be back on Monday."

Alyssa nods before gently tugging it over her head. "How do I look?" she asks, her voice slightly muffled.

Shrupty helps her tuck the edges of the mask under the neckline of her T-shirt. "Not gonna lie," she says. "You're creeping me out."

Alyssa lets out a growl that makes Shrupty scream, then we all burst into laughter. Shrupty slaps Alyssa playfully on the shoulder, but she laughs, too.

. . .

"One more shot and we can wrap," Shrupty says as she crouches down behind the camera. Alyssa yawns under her wolf mask, then starts bouncing on the spot to pump herself up. Hearing her yawn makes me yawn, and then Gabby, too. But not Shrupty—she's been on fire ever since she first said "Action!" hours ago. I always knew she had a talent for making videos; she's been a YouTube star for years. But watching her work, the way she cares about every tiny detail and crafts every second of the scene, I realize I'm witnessing something special.

There's nothing quite like seeing someone doing the work that lights them up from the inside out.

"Okay," she says, clapping her hands together. "Everyone ready?"

Alyssa gets back in position under the fishing net Shrupty borrowed from her dad, then gives the thumbs-up. Shrupty hits record and steps in front of the camera and into her role as Lyla.

Gabby and I are standing on either side of our makeshift set, me holding Shrupty's fold-up light reflector sheet and Gabby manning the ring light. Outside of our little circle of light, the grove is pitch-black. We're like witches making magic in the woods, and I'm loving every second of it.

"Hold it right there!" a deep voice yells from above us. I look up to see a broad-shouldered figure watching us from a trail through the trees.

Shrupty looks at her watch. "Shit. It's ten fifteen."

"Do you have a permit for filming?" he calls.

His flashlight shines down on us as we all look at one another, wide-eyed—except Alyssa, who's still wearing the wolf mask. He trains his light on her.

"What the . . . ," he says.

"Run!" Gabby says, then grabs the ring light and tripod, hugging them to her chest as she races off into the darkness. Alyssa stuffs the net and mask in her backpack and bolts right after Gabby, leaving Shrupty and me standing like deer in headlights.

"Hey!" he yells down at us. "Don't move!" He takes his light off us as he starts making his way down the rocky trail toward us. We see our chance and take it, frantically packing up the last of our equipment and running for the hills.

CHAPTER THIRTY-ONE

We're almost out of the dense wooded area of the park when I trip on a branch and slide down the side of the mountain. Luckily, it's not too steep and I manage to stop against a fallen log. My arms sting from grazing against the rocky terrain, but I don't move.

"Bex!" Shrupty whisper-yells from the trail. "Oh my god! Are you okay?"

"I'm okay," I call back.

"Hold on," she says. "I'm coming."

"No!" I whisper. "Keep going. I'll catch up!"

She ignores me and slowly sidesteps her way down.

I wave a hand up so she can find me, and once she does she crouches down behind the log. "Did you hurt yourself?"

I shake my head. "Don't think so. I'm more worried about the camera equipment."

"It'll be fine," she assures me. "Let's go before he—"

But it's too late. The sound of footsteps approaching makes us sink closer to the ground. Shrupty clutches my arm, and we wait in nervous silence as the guard paces back and forth above us.

A voice crackles through what I assume is his walkie-talkie.

"Hey, Steve," it says. "Any update?"

The guard clears his throat before answering. "I don't see them. I'll keep going, then let you know." His flashlight beams through the trees around us, and I squeeze my eyes shut, hoping he can't see us from where he's standing. After what feels like forever, he continues down the trail.

"What do we do?" Shrupty asks, her voice quiet.

"We have to wait until he comes back this way," I say, peering over the log. "He's on the only trail out of here."

"We're like Frodo and Sam hiding from the Nazgûl," she whispers.

I roll onto my side to face her, resting on my elbow. "I love it when you talk nerdy."

She moves her body closer to mine. "You know one difference between us and that scene from *Lord of the Rings*?" Her voice is low, and I can hear a smile on her lips.

"Um," I say. "We're not hobbits?"

She giggles. "No. They weren't making out."

Shrupty crushes her lips to mine, taking the wind out of

me in the most amazing way. The adrenaline that was already pumping through my veins goes into warp speed. All my senses are heightened. My back presses deeper against the rugged, uneven earth as Shrupty leans over me, running her hands down my waist and onto my hips. Loose strands of her hair fall down the sides of her face, like curtains separating us from the outside world. I breathe in the smell of her shampoo—hints of honey and fig blend with the scents of the pine woods around us. A gentle breeze rolls over us as I wrap my arms around her, kissing her like I've never kissed her before. Like I've never kissed anyone before.

I wish I could take everything about this moment and keep it for the days I feel like I'm hanging on by a thread. The fire I feel right now could keep me warm for a hundred years.

My fingers run through her hair and move up to cradle the back of her head so I can kiss her harder. But our makeout session is interrupted when my phone starts ringing in my back pocket. The tune of the *Silver Falls* theme song echoes through the trees, making us both jump in fright and panic.

"No," I mutter. "No, no, no. Nope. Not happening."

"Quick!" Shrupty whispers as she rolls off me. "He's going to hear it."

I lift my butt up to reach my phone in my back pocket and see Gabby's face on the screen. I slide my thumb over it and answer her call.

"Hey," I say as quietly as I can.

"Where are you?" she asks, her voice high-pitched. She's panicking.

"Hiding," I reply. "Where are you? Is Alyssa with you?"

"Yeah," she says with a sigh. "We're in the car. Did he see you?"

I peek over the log, but there's no sign of him. "Don't think so. But we can't move until he comes back. He's still looking for us."

I hear Gabby updating Alyssa, then she says into the phone, "Should we come find you?"

"No," I say. "He'll see you. Stay in the car and we'll be there as soon as we can sneak out."

"Okay," she says. "Be careful."

"You too." I end the call, and Shrupty rests her head on my shoulder.

"Are they all good?"

"They're at the car," I say as I hold her close to me.

She lets out a sigh. "We're going to be stuck here all night."

I gaze up through the leaves, seeing glimpses of sky and stars. "There's no one I'd rather be lying in the dirt with."

She lifts her head to look at me. "Aww!"

I'm about to pull Shrupty close to me again when a light emerges from the trees above us. We both freeze in place. Footsteps approach down the trail. Shrupty finds my hand

and squeezes it tight. I hold my breath as the beam from the flashlight moves through the trees around us.

"Who's out there?" he calls. My heart races like a hamster on a wheel, and I'm terrified it's beating so loud the whole forest can hear it.

Shrupty and I lay perfectly still, hand in hand, just waiting him out. After a minute or two of eerie silence, we hear the guard speaking into his walkie-talkie.

"Shit," he says. "I lost them. It was just a group of kids screwing around. But I swear one of them had a wolf for a head." Laughter echoes through his walkie-talkie.

"Hey, shut up!" he says. "I know what I saw!" The flashlight switches off, and then we hear his footsteps as he walks away.

"Damn," he mutters to himself. "That's the last time I smoke a joint before my shift." The more his footsteps fade into the distance, the easier I can breathe.

"I think he's gone," I whisper. It's too dark for me to see Shrupty, but I can hear her trying to choke back her laughter.

"Shh," I hush her, but now I feel her shoulders shaking from giggling and I can't hold it in anymore either. I roll onto my side, struggling to keep my laughter at whisper levels. We both lie on the dirt, wheezing and snorting in the darkness. For a fleeting moment, I forget about the sadness inside me. The pain from being fired, from seeing my work taken and misused, from seeing my dreams crushed . . . it all falls away like leaves falling from the branches above us. Something my mom once told me comes to my mind: *Bloom where you are planted.* I must have been six or seven at the time. Mom came home from work with grocery bags hanging off her arms, humming a Backstreet Boys song to herself and smelling like fries.

"Come here, pumpkin," she said as she dumped the bags on the kitchen counter. "Help me unpack these bags."

I remember pouting and dragging my feet into the kitchen, where she pulled out a new fridge magnet she'd found at the dollar store.

"Find a place for this," she instructed me. "Somewhere you'll see it every day."

Then I stood in front of the refrigerator, moving unpaid bills and family photos to the side, and smacked the magnet right in the middle. That's when I read it: BLOOM WHERE YOU ARE PLANTED. It was written in pink lettering over a watercolor sunflower.

"What does it mean?" I asked. I assumed it was another joke magnet, like the one Aunt Laura bought that said THE HIGHER THE HAIR, THE CLOSER TO GOD, but Mom seemed to really like this new one.

She stared at the magnet for a moment, chewing on her bottom lip thoughtfully. "I think it means to be happy where you are, with what you have. You might not be planted in the nicest garden, but that doesn't mean you shouldn't still appreciate what you have and make the most of it."

Maybe I'm high on love fumes, but I think I get it now. My life in LA isn't exactly what I'd hoped it would be, but I'm going to make the most of it. I'm planting new roots right here in this patch of earth above Hollywood, and dammit, I'm going to bloom so hard that this town won't know what hit it.

With fresh determination, I stand up, wipe the dirt off my clothes, and reach a hand down for my girl.

"Let's get out of here," I say.

She takes my hand, and I help her up. "Okay, Frodo."

CHAPTER THIRTY-TWO

"There's a trick to this bitch," I tell Gabby as I slide my key into the front door, just as Parker told me when I arrived in LA. "I'm pretty sure I've finally mastered it." A turn, kick, and thud later, the door opens and I feel like such a champ.

When Gabby, Alyssa, Shrupty, and I step inside, Parker and Dante are on the couch drinking wine and watching *The Rachel Maddow Show*. Parker pauses it and stares at my face, openmouthed.

"What the hell happened to you?" he asks.

I look down at my clothes, covered in dirt and grass stains. "I took a detour down the side of a mountain."

"And I came tumbling after," Shrupty says, inspecting the damage on her shirt. "Sorry for barging in like this. I just need to clean myself up before I go home. My parents will freak if they see me like this."

Parker waves it off. "Don't apologize! Everyone is welcome." He and Dante scoot over so Gabby and Alyssa can sit down. I take Shrupty's hand and lead her into the bathroom so we can get cleaned up.

"I love this apartment," Shrupty says, looking around. "So stylish."

"I know, right?" I say as flip on the light switch and close the door behind us. "Parker has great taste." I turn to her and giggle when I see that the right side of her face is streaked with dirt.

Her eyes widen. "What?" She steps in front of the mirror and laughs when she sees it, too.

I tear open my packet of makeup remover wipes and lift one out. She stands still while I gently slide the wipe over her forehead, down the side of her face, and over her chin.

Shrupty closes her eyes. "Mmm. That feels so nice."

She makes me smile. "You know," I say softly, "a couple of weeks ago, I would have been afraid to invite you here."

"Why?" she asks.

My fingertips touch her cheek as I dab the wipe lightly over her skin. "I was worried you wouldn't like me if you knew I was sleeping on a futon in an apartment that could literally fit into your bedroom."

Shrupty frowns. "Did you think I was that shallow?"

I shake my head. "Not at all. I was obviously projecting my own shit onto you. But I see that now." She opens her eyes, and I push her hair behind her ear. "I know you like me for me."

She looks deep into my eyes. "I really do." Then she leans in and kisses me softly on the mouth, making my heart flutter. "Besides," she adds when she pulls away. "The kind of people who judge you based on where you're from or how much money you have aren't the kind of people you want in your life, anyway."

"Facts," I say as Shrupty takes a wipe from the packet. Then she touches her fingers to my chin, lifts it slightly, and slides the wipe down my cheek. It's cool and soft against my skin as she moves it slowly down my neck.

"Oh," she says, pausing just above my collarbone. "You have a little cut."

"I do?" I turn to the mirror and lift my curls out of the way. A thin red scratch drags down the side of my neck. It's raised slightly, but the skin isn't broken. "Must be from when I fell."

Shrupty stands behind me, looking at it in the reflection. "Ouch. Does it sting?"

I laugh. "I didn't even know it was there." Although now that I'm aware of it, it does start to sting. I open the mirror cabinet to get a Band-Aid while Shrupty gets a fresh wipe.

"I got you, babe," she says, taking the Band-Aid out of my hand. I tilt my head back and she very gently dabs the cut, making me wince a little. I watch her as she cleans my cut, chewing on her bottom lip in concentration. My mind drifts back to Griffith Park, to us lying among the trees far above the world. The electricity between us, the way her body felt against mine . . .

"Are you hot?" she asks, interrupting my thoughts. "You're turning red."

I swallow hard, suddenly self-conscious. "I'm fine." But the energy in the room has shifted, and I find myself breathing heavier, almost like the air is thinning.

Shrupty watches me from behind her long lashes as she peels the Band-Aid from its plastic. Laughter flows from the living room, reminding me that we are not alone. But still, I can't shake the thought of her body underneath mine.

Her fingers brush against my neck as she places the Band-Aid over my cut and smooths down the edges. A shiver runs down my spine. Then she leans in and kisses the space above my collarbone, taking me by surprise.

My heart beats harder as she trails kisses up my neck. She's about to reach my lips when she pulls back, just enough that the tips of our noses graze each other. The corner of her mouth lifts into a sexy half smile, then I close the gap between us. Our lips move together as she takes my face in her hands and I take her hips in mine.

I'm so caught up in kissing her that I don't notice her leading me toward the shower until she's reaching behind her to open the glass door. She tears her mouth away from mine so she can untie her hair from its messy bun. Then watches me with fire in her eyes as she unzips her romper, letting it fall to the floor. My temperature rises, my mouth goes dry. Following her lead, I start unbuttoning my shirt. She smiles as I let it drop to the floor with her romper, then she steps into the shower and turns it on.

It takes me a few seconds to tug my jeans off, but soon I'm leaving my glasses on the counter and stepping in beside her, letting the hot water run down my back. Shrupty drapes her arms over my shoulders, pressing herself against me. We kiss, and the rest of the world fades away. All I see is her.

. . .

When we emerge from the bathroom twenty minutes later, the others are in the middle of what looks to be a very intense game of Jenga.

"No," Parker gasps as he watches Dante reach for one of the middle blocks. He covers his eyes. "I can't watch." Dante's brow is wrinkled in concentration while Gabby and Alyssa watch on the edge of their seats. He's almost got the block out when it collapses all over the coffee table.

"Hey!" Gabby says when she sees us. "You wanna play?"

"I wish I could," Shrupty says, frowning. "But I gotta make it home before my curfew."

Alyssa stands up. "I'll drop you home."

We say our good-byes but linger in the open doorway, neither of us wanting to let go of the other's hand.

"I really should go," Shrupty says, but then she leans in and kisses me.

"Yeah," I say against her lips, then kiss her some more. Then I reluctantly drag myself away from her. "We've got hours *and hours* of video editing to do when we wake up."

She nods. Then smiles and kisses me one more time before letting go of my hand and following Alyssa downstairs. When I close the door, Parker, Dante, and Gabby are all grinning at me.

My cheeks flush. "What?"

"You're in looooove," Parker sings.

CHAPTER THIRTY-THREE

On Friday morning, Shrupty, Gabby, Parker, and I are sitting at our usual table in the garden of the Golden Ivy. We're running on very little sleep, so the coffee is flowing and our anticipation is peaking. I've been so focused on getting this video done that I almost forgot to take my Lexapro, so I wash it down with a glass of OJ.

"I just want to check it one more time before they get here," Shrupty says as she moves her mouse around her laptop screen. Adobe Premiere is open, all our little clips lined up in a row.

Just then, Alyssa and Will arrive, and I wave them over to sit with us.

"Goooooood morning, fellow rebels," Alyssa says with a wink.

They sit across from us, and Gabby claps her hands excitedly. "Are you two ready to see it?"

Will smiles. "Can't wait."

"Come on," Parker says, his eyes pleading with mine. "Let's show them already. I want to see their minds explode."

Shrupty slides the laptop to the side of the table so we can all see the screen. "Here we go." She hits play, and Sasha's boots appear on the screen, hitting the ground as she runs. The next ninety seconds are filled with Lasha's greatest hits from 612. Romantic moments of them caught in a lingering stare fill my heart with emotion. Fast cuts of action shots are sliced between the more tender clips to build tension. Instead of music, Shrupty added the simple sound of a heart beating faster and faster, like a bomb about to explode. And it all ends with a passionate kiss that melts my insides and is guaranteed to make the fans want more. After the last shot fades to black, the words *SAVE LASHA* appear on the screen.

"Whoa," Will says, his eyebrows raised so high they almost disappear into his dark hairline. "That was awesome."

"Fucking crushed it!" Alyssa says before raising her hands up to high-five everyone.

I'm glowing. Seeing something I helped create turn out so brilliantly feels like nothing I've ever felt before. It's not official. It's not even a full episode. And it probably won't ever air on television. But it's ours. We made it.

"I'm so proud of us, gang," I say, beaming.

Shrupty drums her hands on the table, making everything

shake. "Let's post this bitch!" I don't know if it's the caffeine or the excitement that's got her so amped up, but I'm loving it.

Together, we all reach over to the enter button on her laptop, index fingers poised. And then we press it, and the video is officially out in the world.

"Celebration waffles for everyone!" Shrupty yells, throwing her arms in the air triumphantly.

We leave the laptop open on the table while we share waffles and pancakes and even more coffee.

"Look!" Gabby says about thirty minutes after the video went live. "We just hit a thousand views!"

Parker raises his iced cappuccino. "To the rebellion!"

We laugh and clink our glasses and cups to his. "The rebellion!"

We stay until the breakfast rush has dissipated, watching as the view count rises and the notifications pour in from all corners of the internet.

"*Save Lasha* is trending," Shrupty says, scrolling on her phone. "And *HelloGiggles* just shared the trailer with tons of heart-eye emojis."

Alyssa smiles. "It's blowing up even bigger than I thought it would. This has to make Malcolm listen."

"And if not," Will adds, "surely, the network will realize what the fans really want. If Ruby or the board members tell him to cancel the rewrites, he has to do it."

Just then, my phone dings with an e-mail. And so do Shrupty's, Alyssa's, and Will's.

"I guess we're about to find out," Shrupty says. "I just got called to a meeting at the studio."

I check my e-mail and find the same invitation.

Hi Bex,

Ms. Randall would like to meet with you at midday today, if possible.

Please let me know if this works for you.

Angela

"Shit." I hold my phone out so Parker and Gabby can see the e-mail, and their eyes widen as they read it.

"I got it, too," Will says.

Alyssa sighs. "Same."

. . .

"This is fine," Shrupty says as she turns the steering wheel to change lanes. I'd be comforted by her words if it wasn't the fourth time I'd heard her say it since we left the restaurant. I exchange worried glances with Alyssa and Will, who are sitting in the back. Parker and Gabby went back to his place, and right now they're probably on the couch, stress eating and waiting by their phones for updates from me.

"Who knows?" Will says, keeping his tone optimistic. "Maybe she wants to tell us she's bringing queer Lyla back."

Shrupty looks at him in her rearview mirror, nodding. "Yeah. That's it. See? This is fine."

My palms sweat as we pull up to the Rosemount gates. The waffles turn sour in my stomach. My anxiety level is already at a nine, and we haven't even made it into the building yet.

"Whatever happens," Alyssa says, "we stick together. Remember why we did all this—to give queer teens the bad-ass lesbian werewolf romance they've never seen."

We all chuckle, but what she said seems to resonate, because everyone relaxes a little. She's right. This is so much bigger than the four of us.

Angela is at the reception desk when we walk into the building.

"We're here to meet with Ms. Randall," I tell her.

She gives me a sweet smile. "Top floor. But I have a message for you, Bex."

"For me?" I ask, confused.

She nods and picks up a Post-it note from the desk. "Jane would like you to meet her on the soundstage."

"Oh," I say, then look at the others. "I guess I'll meet you up there."

"Okay," Shrupty says before giving me a quick kiss on the cheek that makes me blush. "Hurry."

We go our separate ways, and I run through the lot to meet

with Jane. The doors are closed when I arrive, so I grip the bulky handle and drag it to the side. I'm surprised to find the soundstage empty and eerily quiet. Where is everyone?

"Hello?" I call into the stillness. There's no answer, so I walk inside. "Jane?" The farther into the building I get, the more I feel like something isn't right. I'm about to turn around and leave when the lamp on the living room set switches on.

It's Malcolm. He's sitting in the armchair on set, fingers interlaced in his lap, dark circles under his eyes.

"Is Jane here?" I ask, even though the sinking feeling in my gut tells me she's not, and she's not coming.

"Ruby called you into her office, didn't she?" he asks. "I know she did. Because she called me in, too. Apparently, she's heard some 'concerning things' and wants to 'clear the air.'" He uses finger quotes, then looks at me with daggers in his eyes. "What did you say to her?"

"I didn't say anything."

He stands up from the chair, shaking his head. "People are talking. I know they are. You're turning everyone against me. Everything was fine before you came here." He takes a few steps forward and then stops at the edge of the set. "You know"— he cocks his head to the side—"for such a little thing, you sure do cause a lot of trouble."

I cross my arms over my chest. "Thank you."

"You think you're so smart," he says, walking slowly toward me. "What do I have to do to make you shut up?"

Every cell in my body is telling me to leave. Alarm bells ring in my ears; goose bumps ripple over my arms. Malcolm is a walking, talking red flag, and it's taking everything in me to stand strong against his intimidation. I'm tired of people walking all over me. I'm tired of giving my power away. It's mine.

"Talking to you nicely didn't work," he continues. "Compromising didn't work. Not even my lawyer could keep you quiet."

He stops directly in front of me, then leans forward, towering over me. I instinctively step back, the hairs on the back of my neck standing up. But as I do, I nudge one of the tall, bulky studio cameras facing the set. It gives me an idea.

I raise my palms up. "Please," I say as I hide behind the camera. "Just back off."

He dips his head back to laugh, and I take my chance to turn the camera on while he's not looking. I just hope he doesn't notice the little red light.

"Give me a break," he says. I move around the camera again, maneuvering so that we're both in the shot. He keeps his gaze on me.

"I'm not going to hurt you," he says, his face contorted like he's offended. "I'm trying to help you. Is it money?" He taps his bottom lip thoughtfully. "How much will it take to keep you quiet?"

"Quiet about what?" I ask.

He shrugs. "Everything. If you can go into this meeting

with Randall right now and deny it all—the script stealing, straight-washing Lyla, asking you to sign an NDA—I'll give you whatever you want. Name your price."

"I don't want your money," I say. "You can't buy me."

He pinches the bridge of his nose between his thumb and forefinger. "Why do you have to be so difficult?" He takes in a deep breath, then yells, "Just tell me what the fuck you want so I can move on with my life!"

I swallow hard. I'm not going to lie—I'm afraid. I feel like he's unraveling right in front of me. I glance over my shoulder toward the door. It's still ajar, and if I run I could probably make it. But then I see that red light blinking on the camera, and it spurs me on.

"You know what I want," I say. "Rewrite Lyla to be gay. That's the Lyla I created, that's the Lyla Shrupty signed on to play, and that's the Lyla fans want and deserve. Give the fans what they want. Do the right thing."

Malcolm rolls his eyes. "When are you gonna learn that right and wrong don't matter in Hollywood? All that matters is who has the most power, and that's me. So if you're not going to play nice, neither am I. You either go into that meeting and say what I want you to say, or not only will I ruin you, I'll ruin your pretty little girlfriend, too. All it takes is a phone call, and bam, Shrupty will be blacklisted. Is that what you want?"

I shake my head. He takes a step closer, pointing a finger in my face.

"I can't hear you," he growls.

"No," I say. "I don't want that."

"Then you better keep your goddamn mouth shut," he says. His nostrils flare. "Or I'll have no choice. It's up to you."

He turns and starts walking toward the exit, then calls back to me, "See you at the meeting. Don't be late."

It's not until he walks through the doors that I realize I've been holding my breath. I suck air into my lungs and clutch the camera next to me for support. My fingers start to tremble. My heart pounds in my chest. He just threatened me. He threatened Shrupty.

And I got it all on tape.

I pull my phone out and call Shrupty.

"Where are you?" she says when she answers.

"Shrupty!"

"Bex? Are you okay?" she asks.

"Where are you right now?" I ask, my words spilling out rapidly.

"Still waiting to meet with Ms. Randall," she says. "It doesn't look good for us, babe."

"It's okay," I say. "I just—"

"Ugh," she sighs into the phone. "Malcolm just walked in. We are so screwed."

"I need you to leave," I say.

"What? Why?"

"Just trust me. Meet me in the editing bay."

CHAPTER THIRTY-FOUR

The elevator rises, and so does my blood pressure. I close my eyes and take in a slow, deep breath. Shrupty puts her hands on my shoulders and turns me to face her.

"Open your eyes," she says sternly. I do as she says. "I know this is risky. And fucking scary. I'm scared, too. But we're doing the right thing. How much do you trust me?"

I smirk. "The limit does not exist."

She laughs. "My cute girlfriend just quoted *Mean Girls* to me." She holds her hands in prayer mode and glances up. "I am truly blessed."

Then she traces the back of her hand down my cheek, a gesture so tender and loving that I almost don't know if I can handle it.

"Clear eyes, full heart," she says.

"Can't lose," I say with a smile.

"That's it, babe," she says. "We're going full *Friday Night Lights* on this bitch."

I nod, turn back to face the doors, and straighten my shoulders. I know I should be nervous. I'm about to march into a meeting with one of the most powerful women in Hollywood and tell her that one of her showrunners is trash. And I'm about to do it with him sitting right across from me. So yeah, I should be nervous. I should probably be scared. But I'm not.

I'm fucking pissed.

The elevator doors open, and we step out like Wonder Woman walking into battle. I remember what Alyssa said in the car. This is bigger than us. This is for all the women out there who have been intimidated, bullied, or blackmailed into silence by insecure men trying to hold on to their power. This is for all the *Silver Falls* fans who feel ignored and erased because of decisions Malcolm made.

My rage sits quietly within my chest as the receptionist opens the door to the conference room. Shrupty and I enter to find at least ten white men sitting in a group at one end of the table, and Will and Alyssa on the other end. Some of the men are dressed in suits, others look like they're on the way to the golf course, and all but one of them are on their phones. The one who isn't on his phone is chatting with Malcolm and laughing.

"Ms. Randall will be right in," the receptionist says before closing the door. Shrupty and I exchange confused glances. I feel like we've been thrown to the wolves.

None of the men acknowledge our presence as we take a seat across from them. My stomach turns uneasily. But my rage burns brighter than ever.

The door opens again as Ms. Randall enters. The room falls silent.

"Good morning," she says as she walks past everyone to the empty chair at the head of the table. "Thank you all for coming in on such short notice."

One of the golfers puts his phone on the table and turns to face her. "What's this about?"

Ms. Randall sits down and takes a sip of her coffee. "That's what I'm trying to get to the bottom of, and why I've called you all here this morning."

Malcolm sighs. Loudly.

"Malcolm," Ms. Randall says as she clasps her hands together on the table. "Do you have something to say? A question, perhaps?"

He moves forward in his chair. "It's more of a comment than a question. I just think this whole thing is excessive. When Mark was running this place, he never called me in for meetings with board members present. He stayed out of the trenches altogether. And he would've never called a board meeting with me, cast members, and an intern"—he raises his index finger—"who, by the way, was recently fired for making false accusations and leaking spoilers. I also want to point out that I told you months ago that I prefer not to take on interns, and this is exactly why."

Out of the corner of my eye, I see Shrupty clenching her jaw, like she's literally biting her tongue to stop herself from snapping at him. I take in a deep breath through my nostrils, knowing I need to bide my time. Everything he says just adds more fuel to the fire within me. But I want to do this right, without losing my temper.

The board members all turn to me, but Ms. Randall doesn't take her eyes off Malcolm.

"Well," she says to him. "In case you haven't noticed, I'm not Mark. I wasn't brought in to run this company the same way he or anyone else did it. I'm not afraid of the trenches. And to be honest, I did not want to have this meeting, but your show is falling apart, and it doesn't seem like you're doing anything to stop it, so here we are."

Malcolm crosses his arms over his chest. "Any problems on my show have been caused by one person and one person only."

Oh god. Here we go.

Mr. Randall tilts her head to the side. "And who would that be?"

Malcolm raises his hand and points directly at me, like a witness pointing to the defense in a courtroom. "That girl right there. I'm sure she won't deny any of it, either."

Heat radiates through my whole body. Sweat runs down my back. I've never felt more uncomfortable or more vulnerable in my life. But I've also never been more angry. As I sit at the table, all eyes on me, preparing to defend myself against one of the most powerful men in Hollywood, I remind myself of my power. I am fury, and anyone who stands in my way will feel my wrath.

"Bex," Ms. Randall says. "Why don't you explain your side of all this?"

I nod. "Thank you." I straighten in my chair and initiate eye contact with the people at the table. "First of all, I want to make it clear that I would never do anything to intentionally harm *Silver Falls* or any of the cast or crew. I love this show more than anything."

A couple of the men give me supportive smiles, others already look bored, and Malcolm rolls his eyes.

"You have a funny way of showing it," he says.

Ms. Randall clears her throat. "You said your piece, Malcolm. Let her speak."

Malcolm leans back in his chair, raising his palms up innocently. I gather myself and continue.

"I know Malcolm wants me to say it's all my fault," I say. "He wants me to say that I lied about everything. But I'm not a liar. And I won't be silenced anymore. On the first day of my second week here, he took a script I had written, put his name on it, and handed it out in the writers' room as his own.

When I confronted him about it, he promised to give me a credit, and I let it go. But when I found out he rewrote the character of Lyla to be straight and gave her a romance arc with Archer to help smooth over his homophobia scandal, I had to speak up. After that, I was called into his office, where he and a lawyer tried to pressure me into signing an NDA. They wanted me to tell the world I lied and to support him and Archer. When I refused, he fired me on the spot."

Ms. Randall's eyebrows rise. I pause to take a breath, realizing I may have been talking a little too fast. I'd been avoiding Malcolm's gaze through my whole speech, and when I glance over at him, his face is red with anger. He knows now that cornering me on set didn't scare me. Suddenly, I'm hit with a wave of anxiety, and all I want to do is run out of the room and never come back. But I hold firm, digging my fingers into my thighs and my feet into the carpet.

"Wow," Ms. Randall says. "That's a lot of new information."

"It's all lies," Malcolm says, surprising no one. He throws his arms in the air. "She launched a hate campaign against me and Archer Carlton that has damaged our reputations and the show's success."

"A hate campaign?" Alyssa asks, her nose scrunched up in disgust. "Seriously?"

Malcolm scoffs and shakes his head. "You're part of it." He

turns to Ms. Randall while pointing his finger at Alyssa. "She's part of it! They all are."

Ms. Randall holds a hand up to silence him. She opens her mouth to say something, but one of the suits interrupts her.

"In all fairness to Mal," he says. "He's been showrunner for two seasons, and no one has ever complained about him before."

All the board members chime in then, like a chorus line of mansplaining.

"I've always found him to be a great guy," one says.

"No complaints here," another adds.

"I've known him for years," one of the golfers says with a Cheshire grin. "We go way back. Never had an issue."

Malcolm smacks a hand on the table, like he's been vindicated. "Thank you."

Shrupty and I both roll our eyes. Ms. Randall watches from the end of the table, waiting patiently for the Ping-Pong game of ass-kissing to stop.

"It seems obvious to me," the guy next to Malcolm says, "that the troublemaker in this room is not Malcolm. He's a good guy." Then he pats him on the back.

I want to laugh. Just let out a full-blown belly laugh, right in their faces, to show them how ridiculous and predictable they're being.

"So," Malcolm says. "I think we're done here. If you'll

excuse me, I have a show to run." He stands up from the table. But Ms. Randall is not having it.

She clears her throat. "Excuse me. I say when we are done." He glares at her, but she matches it with her own and he sits down, defeated.

There's a knock on the door, and Jane pokes her head into the room. "Oh, sorry."

Ms. Randall's face softens, and she waves Jane inside. "Everything okay?"

"Um." Jane's brow furrows as she registers all the faces in the room, then she turns her attention back to Ms. Randall. "I just wanted to double-check your notes on this episode, but I can come back." She turns to leave, but Ms. Randall calls her name.

"Take a seat," she says, gesturing to the last available chair, across from me. "I could use your perspective on this whole mess." Then she stands up, fingers poised on the table, and looks over the board. "These are serious complaints that have been brought forward," she says. "And with all due respect to the board, allegations like these should not be swept under the rug or dismissed just because you think he's 'a good guy.'" She shrugs, ignoring the sighs from the board members. "Look, a lot of people in this industry have been held accountable for their bad behavior, but we all know there are so many more who still get away with it. And this is exactly how it happens."

Malcolm shakes his head. "I see how it is." The floor shakes under me, and I realize it's from him tapping his foot nervously under the table. He's scared. "Guilty until proven innocent, huh? Guys like me always get bad rap in the court of public opinion."

"No," Ms. Randall says. "That is not what I'm saying—"

Once again, the verbal Ping-Pong game erupts. I try to interject, to tell them I have receipts and evidence to back up my allegations. But Malcolm's defense team is louder. Shrupty, Alyssa, and Will try to speak up, too, but they're ignored. Jane sits back with wide eyes, looking totally lost. It's like our side of the table is completely invisible.

I fantasize about leaping onto the table, standing over Malcolm, and screaming in his face. I imagine myself getting right up in his face and tearing him to shreds, intimidating him like he's done to me ever since the day we met. In a world with no consequences, I'd let my fury take over and flip the whole damn table.

But the only people who get to live in a world without consequences are men like those sitting in this room. That stops now.

If they won't listen to my voice, fine. I'll give them a voice they'll respond to, one they'll have no choice but to listen to—Malcolm's.

I unlock my phone and open the video Shrupty and I saved. Then I hold it up so everyone can see it, turn the volume up as loud as it can go, and hit play.

CHAPTER THIRTY-FIVE

"How much will it take to keep you quiet?"
Malcolm's voice comes through crystal clear, and the room falls
silent.

I swallow hard when I hear my own voice. *"Quiet about
what?"*

"Everything," the video continues. *"If you can go into this
meeting with Randall right now and deny it all—the script stealing, straight-washing Lyla, asking you to sign an NDA—I'll
give you whatever you want. Name your price."*

I watch Malcolm as his world crumbles around him right
in front of his eyes. Ms. Randall sits back in her chair slowly,
like she's in shock.

"This is a fake!" he yells. The guy next to him puts a
hand on his shoulder and shakes his head at him, and Malcolm
shuts up.

"Why do you have to be so difficult?" The video keeps play-

ing. *"Just tell me what the fuck you want so I can move on with my life!"*

"You know what I want," my voice says. I sound much stronger than I felt. *"Rewrite Lyla to be gay. That's the Lyla I created, that's the Lyla Shrupty signed on to play, and that's the Lyla fans want and deserve. Give the fans what they want. Do the right thing."*

Malcolm drops his face in his hands as everyone listens to him threatening me.

"When are you gonna learn that right and wrong don't matter in Hollywood? All that matters is who has the most power, and that's me. So if you're not going to play nice, neither am I. You either go into that meeting and say what I want you to say, or not only will I ruin you, I'll ruin your pretty little girlfriend, too. All it takes is a phone call, and bam, Shrupty will be blacklisted. Is that what you want?"

Figuring that's all the evidence they need, I stop the video and place my phone on the table. No one says a word for a moment. It's like the air has been sucked from the room.

Shrupty rests a hand on my thigh, squeezing it lightly in support.

Ms. Randall sits perfectly still in her chair, back straight and lips pursed. She looks mad, and I hope to god my plan doesn't backfire and get me in even worse trouble than I'm already in.

"Bex," she says. "When was that video taken?"

"This morning."

She nods, then turns to Malcolm. "Do you have anything to say for yourself?"

He gestures to me. "She obviously coaxed me into saying all that. That girl has been trying to destroy me ever since she walked into my writers' room." No one utters a word. Malcolm searches the faces of the board members for assistance, and they won't even look at him. His face reddens. He leans over to see Jane down at the end of the table. "Jane, come on. Back me up here. You know the truth."

"Yes," Jane says, glancing at me. "I do. And I'm afraid if he keeps running the show, it's going to collapse."

Malcolm jumps to his feet. "What?!"

Jane doesn't even flinch. She ignores Malcolm's antics and looks straight at Ms. Randall. "I've been here since season one, episode one. I went from an assistant to staff writer to story editor to exec producer over my time here. I was even offered the role of showrunner but turned it down because I didn't think I was ready. But that was a mistake. A mistake I've regretted more and more since Malcolm came on as showrunner instead. I firmly believe the recent dip in ratings is because of Malcolm's poor decisions and even worse leadership. And, like Bex, I've had scripts stolen by Malcolm, too. Three so far, all of which I can prove were originally mine."

I have the urge to leap onto the table again, but this time to hug Jane.

Will leans forward. "I agree with Jane." Ms. Randall gestures for him to continue, and he does. "Look, I tried to just sweep it under the rug. I thought letting Mal do his whole chest-thumping routine was standard, as long as the show goes on, you know? But ever since Malcolm took over the show, everyone's on edge. No one wants to cross him in case he blows up. Coming to set every day used to be exciting; we all felt like family. But now everyone is walking on eggshells, too afraid to say anything."

"Alyssa, Shrupty," Ms. Randall says. "Do you feel the same way?"

They both nod. Alyssa folds her arms over her chest. "Personally, I've felt ignored and dismissed by Malcolm ever since I started here. Finding out he sacrificed the first queer romance on *Silver Falls* to protect Archer was the last straw."

Ms. Randall sighs, and her shoulders relax. "Thank you, everyone. I think I've heard—and seen—everything I need to."

Malcolm grits his teeth, seething.

"This is a witch hunt. So I get angry once in a while—so does everyone. I'm not here to make friends, I'm here to get a show done every week, and I've been doing that."

Ms. Randall shakes her head. "Not this week you haven't. Frankly, this whole season has been fraught with problems, long before Bex arrived." She pokes the table with her index finger. "I vowed when I took this job that every show I oversee will be a safe space for all the staff. These scare tactics you seem to employ only damage the show and the network, and we end up here, sitting around a table arguing over who said what and did this or that. I don't have time to be sitting here lecturing you all or playing mediator. That's not my job. But part of your job, as a showrunner, is to keep things rolling and make sure everyone is feeling heard and, most important, that they feel safe coming to work every day. Clearly, you haven't done that. In fact, it seems to me that you've done the opposite."

She looks around the table. "Gentlemen of the board, I propose a vote. All in favor of terminating Malcolm's contract immediately, raise your hands."

Ms. Randall raises her hand. Shrupty's arm shoots up like she's in school, a look of fierce defiance on her face. I raise my hand, too, and so do Alyssa, Will, and even Jane. Our votes may only be a symbolic gesture, but it feels important, and I can't deny how sweet it is to be here to witness Malcolm's comeuppance. Around half of the board members raise their hands, while others seem to hesitate. The guy next to Malcolm cringes and shifts uncomfortably in his seat.

"Brad," Malcolm pleads. "Come on, man. You know me."

Brad avoids eye contact as he reluctantly raises his hand, and the rest of the stragglers do the same.

Malcolm slams his fists on the table, and I almost jump out of my skin.

"This is bullshit!" he yells as he stands up so fast that his chair topples over.

Shrupty and I hold hands under the table. I glance over my shoulder, noting the distance between us and the door.

"Mal," Brad says as he stands up and puts his hands on Malcolm's shoulders. "Calm down, pal."

Ms. Randall presses the intercom on the table. "Call security. Now."

Malcolm shakes Brad off and shoves him, then directs his anger toward Ms. Randall. "That's how it's gonna be, Ruby? After everything I've done for this place?"

Ms. Randall stands firm. "Yes."

He points at her. "I'll sue you!"

She shrugs. "People like you are always surrounded by whispered warnings, Malcolm. I'll be opening an internal investigation into your conduct to turn the volume up on those whispers. So, if you want to sue, go ahead."

The same two security guards who escorted me off the premises the other day burst into the room.

"Please escort Mr. Butler to his office to collect his things," she says to them. "And make sure he leaves without causing a scene."

Brad pats Malcolm on the back. "Come on, bud. I'll walk out with you."

But Malcolm shoves him for the second time. "Fuck off. Fuckin' Judas." Brad backs off, shaking his head.

I sit frozen in my chair as the guards follow him out of the room. He continues ranting and raving in the hall as he leaves the building.

I look around the table at all the shocked faces and catch glares from some of the board members. I can feel their resentment toward me growing by the second. To them, I'm probably just a troublemaking teen. I know how this goes; I'll be labeled as "difficult," and some of these men will make it near impossible for me to work in this town. But I did the right thing; I just need to remember that.

Ms. Randall puts her hands on her hips and sighs. "Thank you, gentlemen. I won't keep you any longer. Leave the rest to me." The board members leave the room, and Ms. Randall turns her attention to our little group of misfits on the other end of the table. I swallow hard and launch into a rambling speech.

"We never meant to cause you so much trouble," I say, stumbling over my words. "We had to take a stand. Not just for us, but for all the *Silver Falls* fans who feel robbed of something they've been wanting for so long. Our methods might be . . . questionable, but I hope you can see now that we weren't just causing trouble for the hell of it."

Alyssa nods. "It was trouble that needed to be made. Trouble that has made the fans feel seen and heard and included in the show like never before."

Shrupty scrolls on her phone and holds it out for us all to

see. "Trouble that has gained over one million views, eighty thousand petition signatures, and inspired op-eds in *Vogue* and the *New York Times*. People want this."

Ms. Randall lifts her hands to quiet us down. "I know all that. And I've known about Malcolm's disruptive behavior for over a month. But the board refused to even hear me out unless I could provide proof. You helped me do that today, so thank you."

I breathe a sigh of relief.

"However," she continues. "Consider this a warning. If you ever share anything about scripts publicly without permission, or go behind the studio's back like that again, I'll have no choice but to fire all of you. And please, come to me if you have any concerns about the people or environment you work with."

Everyone agrees, and with that the meeting is over. Shrupty, Alyssa, Will, and I leave and step into the elevator. The moment the doors slide close, we all start screaming.

"That was the most intense experience of my life," Will says, letting out a sigh of relief.

"It all worked out, though," Alyssa says. She pulls us all into a hug and we stand like that until we reach the ground floor.

"Wait," Shrupty says. "Bex, you didn't get your internship back."

My head hangs a little. "I know. But it's okay. We saved Lyla, that's what matters."

We walk out onto the street and Shrupty stops me. "Wait. If you don't have your internship, what are you going to do?" A frown forms on her face. "You're not going to go back to Westmill, are you?"

"Are you kidding?" I wrap my arms around her waist and lift her up. "How could I leave my girl like that?"

She smiles and kisses me on the forehead. "Good." I let her down and we walk hand in hand through the lot.

"I'll find a job somewhere," I say. "I'm a certified customer service representative, remember? My fast food service skills are the best in the biz. I can work during the day and write at night. Maybe I'll start my own YouTube channel and create my own web series."

Shrupty jumps up and down. "Oh my god, please do that. I'll direct and star in it."

"Bex!" a voice calls from behind us. We spin around to see Jane hurrying after us. She's grinning so wide I can practically see her wisdom teeth.

"What's up?" I ask when she reaches us.

"Oh, nothing," she says, her eyes twinkling. "I just thought you'd want to meet the new *Silver Falls* showrunner."

My jaw drops. Jane points to herself. "It's me!"

"Oh my god!" I say, bringing her in for a hug. "Congratulations!"

She hugs Shrupty, who says, "This is the best news!"

Jane holds her hands over her heart, still grinning from ear to ear. "Thank you. I'm so happy." Her face turns serious, and she taps her index finger on her chin. "But gee. Now that I have all these new responsibilities, I really do need an assistant." She waggles her eyebrows at me. "Do you happen to know anyone who might need a job and wants to work in television?"

My hand shoots straight up in the air like a rocket. "Ooh! Pick me!"

Jane claps her hands. "You're hired. Welcome back!" Her phone rings and she jumps to answer it but pauses to add something else. "You start Monday. See you then!"

Shrupty and I stare after her, slack-jawed.

"Did that just happen?" I whisper to her.

She starts to giggle excitedly, and so do I.

"You're back, Bex!" she says.

I close my eyes to hold back my tears of joy.

I'm back.

CHAPTER THIRTY-SIX

"Are we late?" Alyssa asks as she and Charlie walk through the front door. "Did we miss anything?"

"Just in time," I say as I hand them their party hats. "It's about to start."

They squeeze onto the flattened futon next to Will and Ryan. Parker and Dante drag the kitchen stools over and sit down, while Shrupty, Gabby, and I sit on the floor right in front of the TV.

Shrupty hands me the bowl of popcorn and I take a handful before passing it on. We spent all afternoon getting ready for this. Streamers hang from the ceiling, we decorated the walls with paper flowers, we have popcorn and rainbow cake, and we're all wearing our WE ARE LYLA T-shirts. Everything is set up for a cute watch party.

The alarm on my phone starts ringing, and I squeal. "It's time!"

"Oh my god," Shrupty says, squeezing my hand. "I can't believe this is happening."

The show opens on Sasha's boots hitting the mud as she runs. Jonah and Tom run alongside her. Motorbikes roar in the distance. I remember writing this the night Parker went out on his date with Dante. And now they're here with me, watching it live on national television. Tears brim in my eyes as I think of how I stayed up all night typing as fast as I could, pumping out every scene and watching Lyla come to life on the blank page.

"Here she comes," I say.

Shrupty picks up a cushion and holds it over her face. "I can't look."

Then her face appears on the screen. We all cheer and clap.

"There's my girl!" I squeal. Gabby tugs the cushion down from Shrupty's face.

"You're gonna miss your own debut!" she says, laughing.

Shrupty hugs the cushion to her chest and snuggles closer to me to watch herself save werewolf Sasha from the hunter's trap. The teaser ends and the words *Silver Falls* slice onto the screen behind CGI claw scratches. The opening credits begin and we all sing along to the theme.

When the first scene opens, I lean back and pull Shrupty closer to me, and she rests her head on my shoulder. Warmth spreads from my stomach and all through my body just like it does every time she touches me. I gently kiss the top of her head, and I feel her smile against my shoulder.

"There it is!" Parker screams. He points at the names on the bottom of the screen.

WRITTEN BY JANE SINCLAIR AND BEX PHILLIPS

Shrupty holds her phone up and snaps a photo of it before it fades. I'm smiling so wide it hurts my cheeks, little giggles bubbling out of me. My face must be bright red, and I'm for sure going to spend most of this episode crying, but I don't care. I'm with people who love me no matter how much I drip tears and snot.

Shrupty stretches her arm around me and pulls me into her. "I'm so proud of you."

"I'm so proud of you," I say back to her.

I don't take my eyes off the screen for a second. For the next hour, all of us are enthralled. Mom sends me a selfie of her and Aunt Laura watching the episode back in Westmill with people I used to work with at Sonic. People who didn't even know my name at school a year ago send me friend requests. I decline every single one. If you didn't want me when I was an insecure, closeted nerd girl, you don't get me at my badass, out-and-proud nerd girl.

I can't wait to go in to work tomorrow. This week we're starting to write the special double-episode season finale. The new writing team Jane put together clicked straightaway, and I can't wait to see what they come up with to end season six with a bang. I already know the fans are going to love Lyla as much as I do, so I'm pretty sure Shrupty is going to be signed on for next year. Which is great, because I love being able to see her on set so much—and being able to sneak away during breaks to make out isn't bad either.

The big reveal about Lyla's family is about to hit, and I sneakily watch Gabby and Parker to see their reactions.

"You killed my parents," Lyla growls at her adoptive family of hunters. Parker gasps. Gabby's jaw drops. I'm filled with satisfaction, knowing that this episode is hitting all the beats and giving my favorite people all the feels. I can't wait to jump onto Twitter after this and see what everyone is saying.

The end credits roll, and everyone gets up to dance to the music. Parker goes to the fridge and pulls out a bottle of champagne. We don't have champagne glasses, so Dante gets some plastic Ikea cups out instead.

Shrupty sits on the counter and scrolls social media on her phone. "Lasha is trending," she says with a smile. "Everyone is shipping Lyla and Sasha so hard already!"

The cork shoots out of the bottle with a loud *pop*, and Parker pours the overflow into our cups.

"What should we toast to?" he asks. We all hold our cups in the air.

"To *Silver Falls*!" Alyssa says, and we tap our cups together.

"To queer Lyla!" Shrupty adds, and we toast again.

"To Bex's first writing credit!" Parker says. We toast.

"To the best days," I say, and we cheers a final time.

I take a sip of the champagne. Then we all sit around the coffee table and share the rainbow cake while we watch episode 612 another three times.

If this moment were scripted, I'd fade it out right here.

This is my happy ending.

ACKNOWLEDGMENTS

Just as writing a show like *Silver Falls* is a collaborative process, so is writing a book. I owe so much gratitude to the people who took the time to help craft this story.

Thank you to Jean Feiwel, Lauren Scobell, Emily Settle, Kelsey Marrujo, and the entire team at Swoon Reads for *literally everything*. Seriously, you all work so damn hard and I feel so lucky to be part of the Swoon family.

To my wonderful editor, Holly West, who gets all my geeky references and always knows how to smooth out the wrinkles in the fabric of a story.

To Lauren Spieller, my amazing agent. Thank you for being so very patient, for nudging me forward when I feel stuck, and always looking out for me.

Huge thanks to Britta Lundin for teaching me the ins and outs of a writers' room and life on set. Your advice helped make *Silver Falls* come to life.

Thank you to the sensitivity readers who generously shared their experiences and perspectives to help make these characters feel real.

To one of my oldest, dearest friends, Shrupty. Thank you for letting me name such a cool character after you. Thank you for always bringing out my silly side. And thank you to your parents for all the times they let us have sleepovers on a school night.

To my Mum and Dad, for never making me feel ashamed for loving the things I loved, and for giving me the passion for television and film that inspired this book.

To my Nana, for showing me what a strong female character looks like.

To Rob, for the countless hours we've spent dissecting movies and television since we were kids. Who would've thought we were training ourselves for the stories we tell now?

Special shout-out to Mike, for being the only guy in the cinema for the midnight screening of *New Moon*.

And to Amanda, for being the plot twist I didn't see coming, but now can't imagine my life without. You're my ride-or-die.

Last, but definitely not least, my eternal gratitude goes to all the people who have picked up any of my books. Few things make me as happy as hearing a reader say they connected with my stories. Thank you for letting my characters into your hearts.

DID YOU KNOW...

READER
Swoon
READS
APPROVED

readers like you helped to get this book published?

Join our book-obsessed community and help us discover awesome new writing talent.

1
Write it.
Share your original YA manuscript.

2
Read it.
Discover bright new bookish talent.

3
Share it.
Discuss, rate, and share your faves.

4
Love it.
Help us publish the books you love.

Share your own manuscript or dive between the pages at **swoonreads.com** or by downloading the **Swoon Reads app.**

Check out more books chosen for publication by readers like you.

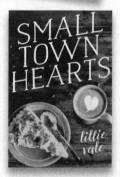
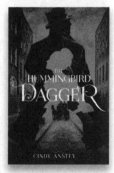